A MATE FOR CHRISTMAS

MOON SHIFTER SERIES

Katie Reus

Cover art: Jaycee of Sweet 'N Spicy Designs
Editor: Julia Ganis
Author website: http://www.katiereus.com

Publisher's Note: This is a work of fiction. Names, characters, places, and incidents are either the products of the author's imagination or used fictitiously, and any resemblance to actual persons, living or dead, or business establishments, organizations or locales is completely coincidental.

A Mate for Christmas/Katie Reus. -- 1st ed.
KR Press, LLC

ISBN-10: 1942447981
ISBN-13: 9781942447986

eISBN: ISBN-13: 9781942447979

For all those who believe in the magic of the holidays.

Praise for the novels of Katie Reus

"...a wild hot ride for readers. The story grabs you and doesn't let go."
—*New York Times* bestselling author, Cynthia Eden

"Has all the right ingredients: a hot couple, evil villains, and a killer action-filled plot. . . . [The] Moon Shifter series is what I call Grade-A entertainment!" —Joyfully Reviewed

"I could not put this book down. . . . Let me be clear that I am not saying that this was a good book *for* a paranormal genre; it was an excellent romance read, *period.*" —All About Romance

"You'll fall in love with Katie's heroes."
—*New York Times* bestselling author, Kaylea Cross

"Reus strikes just the right balance of steamy sexual tension and nail-biting action....This romantic thriller reliably hits every note that fans of the genre will expect." —*Publishers Weekly*

"Prepare yourself for the start of a great new series! . . . I'm excited about reading more about this great group of characters."
—Fresh Fiction

"Wow! This powerful, passionate hero sizzles with sheer deliciousness. I loved every sexy twist of this fun & exhilarating tale. Katie Reus delivers!"
—Carolyn Crane, RITA award winning author

Continued...

CHAPTER ONE

Noel swatted at the garland hanging over the front door. It had fallen from the artful way her oldest sister had looped it over the entryway. She didn't bother fixing it as she stepped outside either. At this point, Ana was lucky Noel hadn't just ripped the whole thing down.

Christmas could go fuck itself.

She was keeping her foul mood to herself, but she was over the holiday and over all this stupid happiness. It was like Ana had decided to make things even cheerier this year to make up for the blackness of last year's Christmas.

Well, Carmen was still dead and Noel couldn't seem to move on. Couldn't be happy. Because if she was happy then it would be a betrayal of her sweet, loving sister who'd been senselessly murdered.

And all around her, people seemed to be celebrating. There had been so many new matings in the last year. Not to mention births and new packmates joining them. She was glad for the births. Cubs were always a joy, but...everything else. It was hard to get excited about.

God, when had she turned into this bitter bitch? She felt as if she'd been simply existing since Carmen died. Just going through the motions and being a "happy" pack member when in reality, she felt like she was suffocating.

Her first mission right now was to move out of the main house. She loved Ana and Connor and was grateful that Ana hadn't moved to another house once she'd gotten mated, but being in the house where Noel had lived with Carmen was too hard lately. Plus she figured that her sister and Alpha wanted privacy. They'd never made her feel as if they wanted her to leave. The opposite, actually. Noel knew Connor must want more alone time with Ana but he'd gone out of his way to make sure she was happy. And not because he was her new Alpha, but because he knew it would matter to Ana. Hard not to love the guy for that alone.

Still...it was time to move. Maybe it was the holidays giving her this sense of urgency, but she knew she needed a change of scenery. A change of something.

It didn't matter that she was surrounded by her pack, surrounded by people who loved her and who she loved in return. She felt so alone. A sort of constant ache resided in her chest. Maybe not constant exactly, but at night when she was alone it was excruciating.

Swallowing back the sadness that seemed to live inside her, she jogged up the steps of one of the new houses on the ranch. At the top she kicked away a mound of snow someone had missed when sweeping off the porch.

Since the Armstrong-Cordona pack had taken in new packmates in the last few months—and others had gotten mated—they'd started building more homes at record speed.

The pack's houses were spread out in circular rings, layered outward with the Alpha's house in the center. It didn't matter that they owned hundreds of acres—the pack lived close together. Though not so near one another that mated couples couldn't have privacy. It was the way most shifters were wired. They needed to be near their people.

She was surprised by how quiet it was when she entered through the open front doorway. There was no actual door installed yet. In the foyer she saw that almost everything had been framed out and most of the drywall was done, but they still had a way to go.

Other than the buzz of a saw from the back of the house, there was no chatter. No banging of hammers. Nothing. Following the buzzing sound, she exited through one of the back door frames—which also had no door installed—and saw Nathan O'Neill cutting a piece of tile.

Her traitorous heart leapt at the sight of him. She started to back away, hoping he wouldn't notice her, but of course he did. Because that was just her damn luck.

The sound died as he turned off the saw and looked up. He shoved his goggles onto his head. "Noel."

God, the way he said her name made everything feminine inside her flare to life. She shoved all those feelings back down. Apart from a few kisses they'd shared a year ago, nothing had happened between them. She'd gone out of her way to avoid him and he sure hadn't come after her, pursued her for more. Clearly she'd meant nothing to him other than some fun. And once things had gotten real, he'd moved on to greener pastures. Or she assumed he had. Not that she could exactly blame him.

She cleared her throat, shoved her hands in her jeans pockets. "Hey. I, uh, I thought Liam was working."

Nathan watched her with steady green eyes. Heading toward her, he tugged his work gloves off. Even the way he walked was sexy, all coiled strength, each move precise. He moved like the predator he was. "He took lunch with December. The others are at lunch too but I wanted to finish up some tile work. Everything okay?"

She swallowed hard as he reached her. Since she was five feet two, most people towered over her, and Nathan was no different. He was broad though. Broad, muscular and very dangerous to her sanity. Wearing work clothes and covered in dust and dirt, he still looked good enough to eat. His hair was a light auburn, his beard the same color. He looked like what she imagined a lumberjack would. He was ridiculously masculine. She inhaled, breathing in the scent of sawdust and something earthy, primal. Something all Nathan that she could never forget. Even if she wanted to.

"I'm good." She took a step back, needing to put distance between them.

His expression softened as he followed. "How are you doing? I know it's hard this time of year for you."

The sincerity of his question ripped something open inside her. She hadn't expected it. Hadn't expected to see him. If she'd known he'd be here she'd have never come. Because simply being around Nathan made her feel weak, needy. She never wanted to be like that for anyone; never wanted to fall for someone so hard that she couldn't live without them. Losing her sister and parents had been hard enough.

She tried to answer around the lump in her throat but was too close to crying. So, coward that she was, she turned on her heel.

"Damn it, Noel." For such a big guy Nathan moved incredibly fast. Even for a shifter. Before she'd taken two steps he'd sidestepped around her, now stood in front of her, blocking her exit.

"What?" she rasped out.

"You're obviously not okay. Do you want to talk about it?"

She shook her head even as she blurted, "I miss her so much." Stupid tears pricked her eyes. Before she could swipe them away she found herself pulled into strong arms.

It had been a long time since she'd been held like this. And the truth was, no one had ever held her the way Nathan was right now. He wrapped his arms around her as if she was precious in a way that was both intimate and protective. Feeling something break inside her, she buried her face against his flannel shirt, wrapping her arms around him as a wave of sadness swept through her. She didn't let any more tears fall, didn't want that dam to break right now. If it did, she wasn't sure she'd stop.

But she still held onto him for dear life. "Christmas is just hard," she whispered, pulling back after a long moment so she could look up at him.

He cupped her cheek with one hand, the feel of his callused palm a shock to her senses. God, she'd been avoiding him for a year because she'd known she'd be weak enough to fall into his arms given the chance. No one had ever looked at her the way Nathan did.

As if he could devour her.

Without thinking she went up on tiptoes. She'd barely moved when he crushed his mouth to hers with an intensity she hadn't expected.

Her entire body flared to life at the feel of his tongue invading her mouth, his huge body pressing her up against the nearest wall.

His cock, already hard, was heavy between them. That was a surprise too, but damn, she liked the feel of it. Moaning, she arched into him, desperate to get as close to him as possible. She didn't want to think about anything. Didn't want to think about how this would probably be a mistake, or how damn guilty she felt for needing to feel pleasure when her sister was gone. She'd never had sex before, but at one time she'd thought Nathan would be her first. That seemed like a lifetime ago. Even if she did regret things later, right now she just wanted to forget everything.

And Nathan could definitely make her forget. She clutched his shoulders, had started to wrap her legs around him when he tore his mouth from hers, took a big step back.

His green eyes flashed with...anger?

Mouth swollen and feeling shaky inside, she stared at him. She was glad the wall supported her. "Why'd you stop?" she rasped out.

His jaw clenched once, a rage she'd never seen from him before flickering in his gaze. "I'm not here for you to use as a way to mute your pain. It's..." He seemed to struggle to speak, all the muscles in his neck pulling taut. "It's screwed up when you know how I feel about you. It's not like you're the only person to lose your pack-mates!" The words were a savage snarl. He turned and stomped out of the house before she could blink.

How he felt about her? What was he talking about? She rushed after him but by the time she'd stepped onto the back porch the only things left were shredded clothes and his shoes. She could see his paw tracks in the light layer of snow, leading toward the woods.

Unexpected guilt punched through her. The pain in his voice and rolling off him in waves had been potent and real.

She wanted to race after him, but if he'd gone running in the forest she'd never find him. Not if he didn't want to be found. Wolves were sneaky like that, able to hide their trail from pursuers.

Feeling out of sorts she sucked in a breath, the cold air seeming icier than normal, cutting at her lungs. A sense of shame invaded her though she wasn't sure why. The only thing she knew was that she had to make this right. She needed to apologize to him at the very least.

Chasing after Nathan wasn't an option, so she headed to December's. The female mated to Liam, the pack's second-in-command, had quickly integrated into their pack and very recently she'd been nicknamed "the secret-keeper." The female seemed to know everything about everyone and if you asked her to keep a confidence, she would.

Noel figured the reason so many of the pack went to December was because after she'd had Elspet—Ellie, for short—her house had opened up to so many visitors. Everyone wanted to see the sweet little cub, and since December baked like a dream, their home had become a natural stopping point during the day for so many.

Noel included. She found herself over there more and more often under the guise of getting baby cuddle time. It made her feel less alone—less sorry for herself. Which was just pathetic.

Rolling her shoulders, she knocked on the door to Liam and December's two-story home. The door would likely be unlocked but she didn't want to intrude, especially since Nathan had said Liam was having lunch with December.

A second later the door swung open. Liam stood there, huge and intimidating, holding a tiny sleeping baby cradled in his arms. Her heart ached at the sight.

"She just fell asleep," he whispered.

"I won't ask to hold her, then... Is December available?"

"Yeah, come on in. You didn't have to knock, you know." He gave her a strange look as he stepped back.

She lifted a shoulder. "I figured you guys might want some alone, grownup time."

He snorted and gently shut the door behind her. "If the door's locked, go away. But if it's not, you're always welcome. You doing okay?" The concern on his face nearly stripped away the rest of her defenses.

She thought she'd been doing a good job of hiding her depression. "Of course. I just wanted to talk to December." She cleared her throat. "Alone." Because she needed to talk to a female who she could trust, and who wasn't her sister. Or one of her cousins. For all Noel knew, they'd feel a need to report back to Ana. She didn't think so but didn't want to take that chance. Ana was her big sister but she was also the Alpha's mate. She had enough to deal with on a daily basis anyway.

Liam kissed her on top of her head and nodded down the hallway. "She's in the kitchen. I'll be upstairs."

Noel found December sitting at the island, a hot cup of cocoa in her hand. The redhead smiled at her. "You hungry?"

Laughing, she shook her head and sat across from her. "I didn't come here for the food." Tapping her finger against the counter, she tried to figure out what to say.

December stood while Noel struggled. Noel watched as she took a pot off the stove and poured some of the contents into another mug. Her mouth watered as she realized it was homemade cocoa, not the packet stuff.

"Whipped cream or marshmallows?" December asked.

"Whipped cream...and some advice. I kissed Nathan," she blurted. "And I think I hurt him. Not physically—obviously." She nearly snorted at the thought. "I just... I don't know what happened. I hurt his feelings or something. But I didn't mean to." The words came pouring out and even if she could stop them, she didn't want to. She'd kept too much buried inside her the past year and it felt as if her heart was just a giant bruise inside her chest. "He made a comment about me using him to erase my own pain, made it sound like...he had deeper feelings for me. And I'm an asshole for hurting him if that's true. I just can't seem to get over Carmen's death. Then I feel guilty because I mourn her even more than my parents. And I feel guilty for wanting to be happy when she's gone, when she'll never experience anything again. It's like I'm all bitter and twisted up inside and I don't know what the hell is wrong with me! Everyone else seems to have moved on from all of our of losses and I can't." Tears burned her eyes, but she didn't let them fall. Her throat was thick, making it hard to swallow.

December set the mug in front of her and wrapped her arms around Noel, pulling her close. Noel buried her face in the female's shoulder and sniffled, letting a few tears escape.

"People cope in different ways. It doesn't mean they've moved on. When you lose a sibling, you don't ever forget. You just learn to live with the pain." December squeezed her once in a tight grip then stepped back, but kept her hands on Noel's shoulders. "I know someone you can talk to. He's a shifter, a doctor."

She frowned for a moment then realized what December meant. "Like a shrink?" She couldn't keep the disdain out of her voice.

December's expression softened as she took a seat next to her. "A psychologist. He's very good at what he does."

"I didn't even know there were shifter psychologists." Who the hell wanted to talk about their feelings to a stranger? She was a lupine, strong, and alpha in nature. She wasn't supposed to need something like that.

December sighed. "Something I've learned in the past year is that so many of our pack and apparently others look down on getting help, whether in the physical sense or emotionally. After Ellie was born I was feeling all out of sorts. Suddenly I had this new, tiny thing who depended on me *and* I could shift into a wolf. I wasn't even depressed, just...sort of a mess of confusion. I talked to Dr. Pomeroy and he made a recommendation."

Noel blinked, beyond surprised. "I had no idea."

She shrugged. "It's not a secret exactly. I just haven't talked about it much, I guess. But I'm not ashamed of needing to speak to a professional."

"Can I ask how Liam felt about it?" Noel thought it might be weird for a mated male to have his mate talk to someone else.

"He was on board with the idea—only after he met the doctor."

Noel bit her bottom lip, contemplating the idea of talking to a shrink. The concept was foreign to her nature, foreign to the way she'd been raised. Before he'd died, her father had been Alpha and insistent that the pack never went to outsiders for help, for anything. Shifters didn't need humans or anyone other than their pack, he'd said. They didn't need anyone for anything. Clearly that attitude wasn't helping her. "Maybe you could give me his information."

December smiled, nodding. "I'll text you everything. And if he's not a fit, there are other shifter doctors you can talk to. I know how hard it is to lose a sibling."

Oh, God. Noel had forgotten that December had lost her brother to a feral shifter. Long before she'd met Liam or moved to Fontana. Reaching out, she squeezed the female's hand. "I forgot, I'm sorry."

"Don't be. I'm just letting you know you're not alone."

"I actually know that." Literally all of her packmates had lost someone. "I just... Gah, I don't know. I feel like everyone is moving on but me. Then today with Nathan... What?" she asked when December gave her a pointed look.

"I probably shouldn't say anything, but I see the way Nathan watches you, follows you around. He's even asked that his patrol shifts be scheduled so that he's off when you are. I don't know him well though, so..." She lifted her shoulders. "I just know that he wants to be off when you are. Make of that what you will."

Stunned, Noel digested the words. After Nathan and she had shared a few hot kisses everything in her life had gone to shit. She'd cut him out of her life, but he'd never pursued her, never...done anything. She'd just assumed he'd been having fun with her because clearly he hadn't wanted more. Then when things had gotten hard, she'd assumed she'd been too much of a hassle for him to deal with.

Maybe she'd been wrong.

CHAPTER TWO

Nathan stared blindly at the words in front of him, not comprehending anything. The cabin was too quiet and his mind was too mixed up to read anything. Sighing, he set the book down and rubbed a hand over his face.

What had once been the single guys' cabin housed pretty much just him and two others now. Liam had moved out when he mated with December. Noah had moved out soon after mating with Erin. Ryan had done the same when he and Teresa had mated, taking Lucas, his adopted cub with them. Even Rafael, who'd only been with them for a short time, had moved out after mating with Rosa.

Nathan had thought those two were mismatched, given the disparity in their personalities, her being so beta and him being so very alpha. But Rafael was completely smitten and would do anything that female asked.

And Nathan was jealous. All his friends were mated and he couldn't have the one female he wanted.

The only males left were Jacob and Lucero, who was the newest member of their pack. But they were out on patrol tonight. So he was alone, ready to crawl out of his skin after what had happened today with Noel.

He'd been pretty much obsessed with her for the past year. But he might as well have been invisible. She hadn't seen him. Or hadn't wanted to. It was as if what they'd shared had meant nothing to her. They'd only kissed and spent a few days together but it had sure meant something to him. He'd tried to comfort her after Carmen had died, tried to be there for her. But she'd cut him off and after a while he'd realized that she was simply avoiding him. That had sliced deep.

The thing was, he understood why she hadn't wanted to see him at first. Since her sister died, she'd been like a ghost of the woman he'd first met. He'd been giving her time, letting her grieve in her own way.

Because he understood. He'd lost his family too. And it had taken him a long damn time to come to terms with it.

In spite of his efforts, Noel had started avoiding him after a few months. Then for her to come to him to ease her pain today, knowing how he felt about her? It was cruel. It went against everything he knew about the female.

When he heard a tentative knock on the door he shoved up from his chair. He was barely halfway across the room when he scented *her*. That exotic mix of deep amber and vanilla. It made him still for a moment before gritting his teeth and bracing himself for what seeing her would do to him. Everyone had a unique scent, and shifters and other supernaturals were more attuned to it than humans.

He opened the door to find Noel in jeans, knee-high boots, a berry-colored sweater and a fitted black leather jacket. Her long, dark hair was loose around her face and shoulders in soft waves. Just seeing her was a punch to all his senses.

"Do you have time to talk?" Her voice was low and there were too many emotions in her bright amber eyes for him to decipher.

Nodding, he stepped back to let her in. No matter what, he simply couldn't seem to say no to her. Her amber and vanilla scent wrapped around him, suffocated him.

Fuck. He didn't *want* to want her. Not when it was clear she didn't feel the same about him.

She wrung her hands in front of her, clearly uncomfortable. He knew he should offer her a seat or a drink or something, but couldn't make his voice work. All he could do was stare. And hate himself for wanting her so desperately.

"I owe you an apology. I...kissed you because I wanted to, but I also kissed you because..." She swallowed hard, clearing her throat. "I thought it would help me forget for a little bit. I wasn't trying to use you though. Not really. I mean, well, I guess technically I was. But I thought...since we had fun before, you'd be into it. I wasn't trying to hurt you or be malicious."

"Fun?" he rasped out. Is that what she thought?

Her eyes held a hint of panic. "I assumed it was just fun for you. After Carmen died and I pretty much lost it, you never came after me. Never came to see me." Her voice cracked with clear hurt. "Until today I didn't think what we'd shared even mattered to you."

Her words were like a blade going through his chest. "You don't get to rewrite history," he rasped out, anger and pain battling inside him.

She blinked, her confusion so crystal clear that the blade drove deeper. "What?"

"I *did* try to comfort you. I was at the main house every day for a month. You didn't want to see me, didn't want to see anyone except your family."

She dropped her hands. "You were?"

Surprise ricocheted through him. He'd assumed she'd known. "Yes." He'd waited like a puppy for her. "You didn't know?"

"No."

The truth rolled off her in a subtle wave. She couldn't have lied to him even if she'd wanted to, not with his scent abilities.

He scrubbed a hand over the back of his neck. Clearly they needed to hash some stuff out, and standing here in the middle of the foyer wasn't the place. He locked the front door so if anyone decided to stop by they'd know to leave. He didn't want any interruptions, no matter how small. "You want to sit?"

Letting out a sigh of relief, she nodded. "Yes."

In the living room she sat on one of the smaller stuffed chairs so he sat on the loveseat closest to her. Some primal part of him still needed to be as close to her as possible, no matter how much she'd hurt him. A fire crackled behind her, giving her coffee-colored hair a soft glow.

"When you said it was screwed up, what I did... Kissing you, when I knew how you felt about me... What exactly did you mean?" Her voice was soft, her words tentative.

Yeah, he wasn't going to answer that. He'd assumed she'd known, assumed that was why she'd avoided him. That she didn't reciprocate his feelings so she'd decided to just ignore him. "You really didn't know I'd come to see you all those times?" He needed to hear her say the actual words.

She shook her head, her expression filled with pain. "No, I swear it. With everything going on with the APL back then and losing Carmen, I just... Everything is sort of a haze. I was just going through the motions of existing." Her voice cracked again.

Ah, hell, it went against all his survival instincts where she was concerned but he moved lightning fast and knelt in front of her. He gently took her hands in his. His wolf instantly calmed when she didn't pull away. "I didn't think you wanted me around. I thought you were avoiding me. Or I would have been there for you." Maybe he hadn't tried hard enough. He thought he'd been giving her the space she needed to mourn.

"I...did avoid you, later." She whispered the words, anguish etched in every line of her face. "I thought you'd brushed me off when you never came to see me—when I *thought* you didn't—and I knew I'd be weak where you were concerned. I didn't want to use you as a crutch and get even more hurt when things ended between us."

"*When?*" he growled. What the hell did that mean?

She didn't respond one way or another.

What the hell. There would be no *when* where she was concerned. Never. Everything she was saying screwed up his whole world right now. She hadn't known about his feelings for her and hadn't intentionally been cruel earlier today. This put everything into a whole new perspective.

It was clear she was still mourning though. Didn't matter. Starting now, he wasn't going to lose her a second time. He simply couldn't.

There was a lot he still wanted to say to her, but if he told her how he truly felt, he'd probably scare her off. Especially since she wasn't giving him anything to indicate she wanted a relationship from him right now. He had to take things slow, do things right this time. But no more blending into the background, no more letting her mourn alone. "Do you have plans tonight?"

She blinked, clearly surprised by the abrupt change in topic. "Ah, no."

"I was going to head into town, look at the lights. Want to come with me?" What he wouldn't give to lean in closer to her, to nibble along her jaw, devour her mouth—pin her underneath him in front of the fire and make her moan his name.

"Ah..." She squeezed his hands briefly before pulling her hands away. "I'm a mess right now, Nathan. I don't want to give you the wrong idea."

"We can be friends, right? I'm just a packmate asking another packmate out for a walk and maybe drinks." He almost choked on the words. The truth was, he wanted her friendship as much as he wanted her for his mate. He wanted everything from her. Even if she wasn't ready for more than friendship right now, he knew she was physically attracted to him. She couldn't hide that, and the kiss from her this afternoon had been real.

It was a start.

She half-smiled, the tension in her shoulders easing. "Of course. I really am sorry about earlier. I wasn't—"

"I know. We probably should have talked a long time ago." He should have just gone to her even though he'd known she was avoiding him. Maybe it would have made a difference.

"Yeah. So...we can be friends?" There was a hopeful spark in her eyes.

He nodded and even though he did want her friendship, he planned to claim a lot more.

* * *

As Nathan parked his truck along the curb on Main Street, Noel wasn't so sure she should have agreed to go out with him—but saying no had been impossible. Even if she wanted to keep her distance, that kiss they'd shared had reawakened something inside her.

Made her feel alive, as if the veil over her eyes had been lifted after so long.

She'd had no idea he'd come to see her all those times after Carmen died. Neither Ana nor Connor had said anything, and the truth was, things had been insane back then. The pack had been dealing with the Antiparanormal League—a bunch of crazy racists who hated anyone paranormal or different than them—as well as integrating Connor's band of males into their female pack. And a whole bunch of other stuff she could barely remember. Their lives had been in a constant state of upheaval then. To know Nathan had wanted to be there for her had pretty much screwed up everything she thought she knew about him, about what they'd shared.

Now she felt all awkward and unsure of herself. She desperately wanted him, had been more hurt than she wanted to admit when she thought he hadn't been there for her. But she was still a mess inside. Starting something with Nathan would be stupid. He didn't deserve a broken female. He was right though; they could be friends.

Unfortunately, when she looked at him she didn't see someone she wanted to be friends with. She saw a sexy, broad-shouldered male she wanted to strip naked with and go skin to skin.

Yeah, being friends should be no problem.

"You want to stop by Growling Bear?" Noel asked as they stepped onto the sidewalk together. It was a little shop owned by humans, Kaya and her son, Matt. The Native American family had been the first to accept the Cordona pack when shifters and vampires had revealed their existence to the world over twenty years ago. The Cordonas had already been living in Fontana, had carved out a home for themselves. Not everyone had been accepting, but they had.

"They closed up early tonight." He fell in step with her. Everything about him screamed sex appeal. As if he should be carrying around an axe and chopping down trees. Or running into a burning building to save people. She wasn't the only one who noticed, she realized, as they started down the brightly lit sidewalk. Women's gazes gravitated to him, lingered for a second or two longer than was necessary.

She frowned, not liking how many women seemed to notice him. "How do you know that?"

He lifted a shoulder. "I overheard Eva telling one of her sisters that she was meeting with Matt. That was over an hour ago."

"Ah, of course." Noel had heard through the grapevine that her cousin Eva and Matoskah Dunlauxe—

Matt—had started seeing each other in the last month. His mother Kaya would be so thrilled he'd found happiness with someone. "I think we'll have a new mating soon enough." She remembered how Carmen had used to flirt with Matt, and that vise tightened around her chest.

"What is it?" Nathan murmured, sliding his arm around her shoulders.

The action should surprise her, but shifters needed touch by nature. He was just being friendly. She wouldn't read anything into it. Even if his simple hold soothed her, made her want to bury her face against his neck and inhale his masculine, earthy scent. "It's nothing."

He squeezed her shoulders once. His natural scent made her lightheaded, hungry for him.

God, she really needed to keep her head on straight. "I just remembered how Carmen used to flirt with Matt. She'd been so smitten by him. I think of her at the most random times."

He squeezed again. "It's okay to talk about her— you *should* talk about her."

The light poles lining the street were lit up with white and red Christmas lights. Big sparkly candy cane lights topped each pole. Though it was close to seven, most shops were still open. The scents and pretty, glittery things in the windows were a siren's call to anyone passing by. Well, anyone but her. She was over all the Christmas crap everywhere.

"December mentioned that I could maybe talk to a...therapist or something." She felt stupid even saying the words, was already cringing while she awaited his reaction.

"That's not a bad idea." He looked down at her as they came to the end of the sidewalk, waiting for the crosswalk light to turn.

"Really?"

"Sometimes it's easier to talk to a stranger. But I'm here if you need me. Always."

"Thank you." He was telling the truth. A male like Nathan wouldn't offer anything without meaning it. That knowledge stirred something else inside her. Something she didn't want to evaluate too deeply.

They walked down the main strip in silence, taking in the lights and people. Before losing Carmen, Christmas had been Noel's favorite time of year.

"Where are we going, anyway?" she asked after five minutes of walking. On the drive downtown he'd said their final destination was a surprise, but she was not a patient she-wolf.

His lips quirked up. "You'll see."

"I hate surprises."

He just gave her a smile that made her think of all sorts of wicked things they could be doing right now. For the first time in a year she felt almost alive again. As if the cloud that she'd been living in had finally lifted a bit.

They turned a corner at the end of the strip and she instantly realized where they were going. Behind the main strip of stores and before the local high school there was a huge skating rink. "For some reason I can't see you ice skating."

"Ah, yeah, *I'm* not going to." His boots thudded softly against the sidewalk as they crossed the street.

Laughter and Christmas music filled the air as they reached the other side. The outside rink had a thick glass enclosure surrounding it and a pretty white picket fence framed the rest of the huge area. "You're going to make me skate by myself?" She bumped him with her hip as they headed down one of the sidewalks that led to the rental booth and vendor cart.

He stopped when they reached the line for hot cocoa. "I'll give support from the sidelines."

"No way. You're doing it with me. With your genes, I know you'll be fine." She didn't want to come out and say 'shifter genes.' While most humans in town seemed to accept them, she knew that not everyone loved shifters. She didn't want to announce who they were.

He gave her a dubious look that made her laugh.

"You can hold my hand for balance."

Heat spread through her like wildfire at the hungry look he gave her. It was so quick she might have imagined it, but she knew she hadn't.

Before either of them could say anything, the human woman in front of them with curly gray hair peeking out from her white and red knit cap half turned and gave Nathan a big smile. "And if you really need the help, I'll hold your other hand." She had to be in her sixties, maybe seventies.

Noel smothered a laugh and just grinned as Nathan actually blushed. He mumbled a non-response to the adorable woman and ended up paying for her hot cocoa as well as theirs.

Once they were alone sitting on one of the benches, Noel erased any distance between them and sidled up next to him. His masculine, earthy scent was heaven and a little bit of torture. A year ago she'd thought they might have something real. Then when things had gone to hell and she'd assumed he wanted nothing but fun from her, it had been easy to cut him out of her life, to pretend they'd never shared those intense kisses behind the barn.

She looked at his strong profile. His light auburn hair was a little long—definitely long enough that she could run her fingers through it. She kept her hands firmly around her warm cup. "Can I ask you about something you said earlier?" It had been bothering her all day.

He met her gaze, nodded.

"You said I wasn't the only person to lose packmates... Did you lose someone before joining with Connor?" She knew he must have. Almost all shifters over a certain age had lost someone to violence—or even human friends to old age.

His green eyes seemed to darken before he looked away, staring out at the rink. A thick sense of joy seemed to fill the air, everyone in the holiday spirit. Two years ago she would have been in the holiday spirit but now it was a like there was a dark cloud over Christmas.

"I wasn't part of a big pack. It was my parents, brother, and two other mated couples. Eighty years ago things were different."

She nodded. She was only sixty and she'd been very sheltered growing up. But she understood what he meant. Eighty years ago they hadn't yet come out to humans, so things were very different. Most packs had been small and even the bigger packs had been insulated from humans. A necessity because they'd had to move every couple decades.

"Vampires wanted the land we owned." His jaw tightened and she knew what was coming even before he said the words.

It was a common story among shifters and vampires. One of the most common, in fact. There had been so much death and bloodshed between their species decades ago. Mostly before her time, though there were still squabbles now and then. She slid her arm through his as he talked, wanting to touch him.

"I was the only one who survived."

Her throat tightened at his words. Squeezing his arm, she laid her head on his shoulder. "I'm so sorry." He'd lost his brother and parents, something she unfortunately could understand. Losing packmates was one of the hardest things. Losing family members was even harder.

He leaned his cheek against the top of her head. "I didn't have anyone to talk to for a long time. No one who would get it. I was barely a full-grown male when I lost them. When Connor found me and put together his pack, it changed everything. Gave me a purpose. I'm not saying losing them gets easier, but time makes a difference."

She wished she could take away the lingering pain she sensed rolling off him. It wasn't harsh or overbearing, just a subtle scent in the air. But it was enough to make her wolf agitated. She'd been so caught up in her own grief she hadn't noticed that others might be hurting too.

The truth was, she hadn't wanted to notice. She'd been consumed with her own needs. Now...the thought of Nathan in pain made her want to comfort him. Okay, she wanted to do way more than comfort him.

CHAPTER THREE

"Is that Noel and Nathan?" Ana squeezed Connor's hand as they strolled along the walkway that encircled the skating rink. "They're holding hands," she said before he could respond to what was basically a rhetorical question anyway.

Her mate chuckled, the deep sound wrapping around her. "Yeah, I heard he was taking her out tonight."

"And you didn't tell me?" Her sister had been in a funk lately and it had been starting to worry Ana. She'd already lost one sister. She wouldn't lose Noel.

"One of the pack texted me as we were leaving. But...I should tell you I think she's going to want to move out soon."

"Because of Nathan?"

Her tall, sexy mate shook his head. "Maybe eventually, but no. I just have a feeling she wants to get out on her own. Away from us."

Yeah, Ana had been getting that vibe from her younger sister lately too. "I don't know if it's a good idea." Under any other circumstances she'd have been happy her sister wanted to spread her wings, but she didn't want Noel moving and isolating herself even more. Not when she'd been withdrawing into herself.

"I agree. What do you think about Niko's plan?" Connor asked, abruptly changing the subject.

Which was his way, she'd discovered in the last year. As Alpha he had a lot to deal with on a daily basis and he discussed everything with her. She loved that there weren't secrets between them, that they were a team. "I think he needs to tell Gloria before she claws his eyes out."

Connor snorted. "No kidding." He dropped her hand and quickly wrapped an arm around her shoulders as they headed away from the rink and deeper into the park.

Ana was so glad they'd managed to sneak an evening away. For once the stars had aligned in their favor. "I think it's a great idea what he's planning. I'll miss her but...she deserves to see the world." Gloria was a beta and one of the backbone of their pack, but they'd survive without her for a little while.

Connor's big hand slid up her waist and higher as he not-so-subtly cupped her breast. She had on a red cashmere sweater and a black peacoat but she could feel the heat of him even with all the layers of clothing.

She shifted slightly, looking over her shoulder at the empty sidewalk behind them. "Planning on getting frisky out here?" she murmured, turning fully into him.

"Maybe," he murmured, bending his head toward hers.

As his kiss deepened, his tongue teasing her own, she automatically leaned into him, wanted to wrap her body around his. Then an unfamiliar scent made them pull back from each other almost at the same time.

She turned to see a human couple coming from the direction of the park, laughing and holding hands, oblivious to anyone around them. A part of Ana envied people who didn't have to be on guard all the time.

Even out here with her mate, she knew that they couldn't truly let their guard down. They couldn't grab a quickie in the park even if she really, really wanted to get a little wild with her mate right now. She didn't even care that there was a light layer of snow on the ground. Sometimes her wolf side wanted to throw caution to the wind and revel in her sensuality, her more primal side.

Sighing, Connor wrapped his arms around her shoulders again. "I say we find a place to park on our land instead of going home right away."

"Is 'park' code for something else?" She wrapped her arm snugly around his waist.

"Definitely." The word was a soft growl before he kissed the top of her head.

A shiver of anticipation streaked through her. She loved when he got all growly. "So who do you think will get mated next?" she asked a few minutes later as they headed back downtown to where they'd left their truck.

Energy hummed through her. She was ready to feel her mate's hands on her, to be skin to skin, and couldn't wait much longer.

"Matt and Eva."

Ana nodded. "I think so too." At one time Connor hadn't liked Matt, had thought he was a threat to the pack. That seemed like a lifetime ago instead of just a year. It was hard to believe how much things had changed in so short a time.

"It'll be good for the pack too." His voice was matter-of-fact.

She understood what he meant. If one of their packmates mated with a human with strong ties to the community, it would be positive for their image. She hated that they even had to think in those shallow, political terms, but it was a fact of their lives. They had to care about image to survive in this world. Liam mating with December—the sheriff's sister—had ended up being a very good thing for the pack.

"And I like to think that Noel and Nathan will get together too." She hoped so anyway. She wanted her sister to be truly happy.

Connor didn't say anything, just pulled her closer as they turned onto Main Street. When they passed a children's clothing shop, Ana's heart rate increased the tiniest bit. Though she tried to hide her reaction, her mate missed nothing.

"What?" Connor frowned down at her.

She gave him what she hoped was her most wicked grin. "Just thinking about the 'parking' we'll be doing soon." Which was mostly true.

She never lied to Connor but right now there was something she still wanted to keep to herself. Just for a few more days. She would tell him on Christmas morning. At least that was her plan.

After taking a dozen tests, she was certain she was pregnant. And her doctor's appointment had only confirmed it. During her last heat he'd worn condoms because she didn't think they were ready for cubs. Looked like they were going to have to get ready.

Right about now she was pretty freaked out. Things had finally settled down at the ranch and the thought of bringing a cub into this world terrified her. Not only that, but the Alpha having a child was a big deal. Their baby could be targeted simply because he or she was Connor's.

Still…a bubble of excitement had started to grow inside her at the thought of having a baby, of holding a cub of her own. She'd basically been a mom to so many of her cousins over the years, and the thought of having a cub that she and Connor had created together?

Yeah, pretty amazing. Still, when she told her mate they were going to have a baby, she wanted to have her head fully wrapped around the fact that their lives were about to drastically change.

* * *

Nathan grasped Noel's smaller hand in his. She was petite and though she looked fragile, he knew she wasn't.

Strength hummed through her and he felt the subtlety of it in her hold.

As they glided around the skating rink, he had no problem holding her hand for balance. He was a freaking warrior, trained through and through. And he was an apex predator.

Balance was not a problem for him.

But if he got to hold Noel's hand? Then he could be a terrible skater for the next couple hours. They'd been out here for an hour already, talking, skating and taking hot cocoa breaks.

Her cheeks were flushed pink when she looked over at him. God, what he wouldn't give to see her look like that under different circumstances. To see her hair tousled around her face, her cheeks all red after he'd made her come against his tongue. He wondered what she would taste like, how responsive she'd be. He shifted uncomfortably, trying to get his body under control.

"What? You need a break?"

"Yeah, maybe on one of those benches over there." His gaze fell to her mouth again, but he quickly looked away. Focusing on her perfect, lush lips wasn't conducive to keeping his body under control.

As they reached the farthest section of the elongated skating rink and the benches he'd been talking about, he moved a little closer to her. He wanted more than to just hold her hand. He wanted to pull her to him, to feel her underneath him, skin to skin. No barriers.

Turning to the cluster of empty benches, the front edge of his blade caught on the ice. As he pitched forward, Noel grabbed onto him. He wrapped his arms around her and twisted so that his body would take the brunt of the impact. He probably could have righted himself, but damn it, he wanted to feel her against him and would take any excuse he could.

As they tumbled into a fluffy section of snow between two empty benches, she let out a squeal of surprise and spread her hands over his shoulders as she pushed up slightly. "Are you okay?"

He couldn't answer as he stared up at her. It was impossible to find his voice with her body tangled with his. Her bright amber eyes glowed ever so slightly, her expression pure joy, and for a brief moment he was reminded of the first time he'd kissed her in the pack's barn. He'd pressed her right up against one of the stall doors and she'd wrapped her legs around his waist, urging him to do more than just kiss her.

Now, when his only answer was his growing erection, she sucked in a breath, her fingers digging into his shoulders. Her breathing grew erratic, her pupils dilating as she stared at him.

Laughter and the sounds of others skating nearby filled the air, but they were far enough away from the majority of the people that no one could see them.

"I want to feel you under me, want to be skin to skin," he rasped out.

Her eyes widened as she sucked in a breath. "Nathan..."

"We have chemistry." Because screw simple friendship. He'd take it if that was truly all she wanted, but she couldn't deny the electric energy that seemed to spark between them.

The dark scent of her heat tinged the air, her arousal making him lightheaded. "That might be true, but I wasn't kidding when I said I'm a mess. It would feel too much like I'm using you for something physical."

"So?" Saying the word gutted him, but the truth was, he'd take her how he could get her. It didn't matter what he'd told her before, that he didn't want to be used. This was his opportunity to reel her in. He'd make it so good for her she wouldn't be able to stay away. It was a starting point to winning her heart anyway.

She blinked.

"I'm okay if you want to use me." Not exactly a lie as he leaned down to brush his lips over hers. All the thoughts he'd had of going slow dissipated as her mouth parted under his on a soft, acquiescing sigh.

His tongue flicked against hers, and in the back of his head he knew he needed to pull back before this went too far. But his wolf refused to listen.

Noel pulled back suddenly, her cheeks a darker shade of red than before. "I'm not okay using you," she whispered even though he could scent her desire.

"Noel—"

A terrified scream rent the air.

"Help!" A young male voice yelled again.

Nathan was up on his skates in seconds, pulling Noel up with him as another scream filled the air.

"There!" Noel shouted, unlacing her skates as he did the same.

Past the skating rink guard, a small child was on the edge of a small frozen pond—and someone must have fallen in, given the splashing and muted cries for help.

Without pause the two of them jumped over the railing of the rink. It might be freezing out, but he barely felt the cold through his socks, and Noel wouldn't either due to their higher body temperatures. Even if he'd been able to feel the icy cold, he'd still be helping.

"Help my sisters!" The boy continued screaming, his terror raw, palpable, urging Nathan on.

"You swim?" he asked Noel even though he figured she did.

"Yeah." Her breathing rate had increased but she kept pace with him, racing over the fluffy snow. "He said sisters. There might be two of them."

He'd caught that too. Nathan stripped off his jacket and shirt as they neared the bank of the pond, ignored the cries of the boy who was in a clear panic, just screaming now. There were other shouts of alarm far behind them but he tuned those out too.

The icy surface of the pond chilled his feet as he skidded out onto it. The majority of it was frozen but cracks splintered out over the surface in areas.

"The hole is icing over." Noel's voice filled with panic as she followed him.

There was no more splashing and his own fear for the safety of the girls in the pond ratcheted up his heart rate. No one was dying here today. No parent was going to bury their children.

The need to protect, to help, drove him on, Noel a steady presence at his side. A crescent moon illuminated the icy surface as they moved out deeper and deeper into the middle.

The ice cracked beneath his feet and they both stilled, scanning for signs of life. No one should have been on this pond. Clearly the kids had ignored the posted signs. Not that it mattered. They were freaking kids and needed help.

"There," Noel murmured, pointing to a flash of pink under the surface of the ice.

Two little girls were flailing under the now iced-over hole, one just barely moving her hands.

They moved as a unit, ignoring the continuing cracks as they hurried over the ice. Two sets of hands pressed up underneath the ice, the fear in the girls' eyes clawing at him.

He crouched down on the ice. "We need to break through. But they're not going to understand when we tell them to move back." Because they were maybe ten years old and were terrified out of their minds—and likely close to hypothermia and drowning.

"I'll break through on the right, next to this girl," Noel said, lifting back a fist, not waiting for him.

Doing the same a few feet away, Nathan slammed his fist into the ice, smashing through it like glass. His knuckles split but he ignored the pain. He pounded and pounded until it gave way beneath him. Out of the corner of his eye he was aware of Noel doing the same.

Icy water rushed over him as he fell into the pond, all the muscles in his body tightening in a natural instinct to save warmth as he wrapped an arm around a limp little girl. *No, no, no.* He would get her out of here.

"I've got this one!" Noel was shoving a barely conscious girl in all pink onto a solid slab of ice. The girl's teeth chattered as Noel climbed up behind her and it was clear she was breathing.

Moving quickly, Nathan did the same. Moments later they both scooped the girls up and started making their way back to shore. Even though he wanted to sprint, he was very aware of the cracking—too much pressure and they'd go right back in.

"Stay back!" he shouted to the little boy who'd stopped crying but looked as if he was ready to rush onto the ice. A crowd of people were running over the snow toward them.

Not for the first time he realized how much slower, weaker humans were. It was as if they were moving in slow motion.

"Can you hold her for a sec?" Noel asked the sniffling boy as Nathan stretched the other little girl out onto her back. The girl Noel had saved was breathing, but the one he had wasn't.

They needed to get them out of their wet clothes, but first, he had to save this little girl.

He was aware of Noel grabbing her previously discarded jacket and wrapping it around the shivering girl she'd saved as he started doing chest compressions and CPR on the human who looked impossibly fragile.

He checked her pulse. Nothing. His heart was in his throat as he started doing chest compressions. *One, two, three.* Nothing, damn it.

No, no, no. She couldn't die. He wouldn't let it happen. *One, two, three*—sucking in a breath, the little girl jerked and coughed out a handful of water. He rolled her onto her side, helping her cough it out.

Now they needed to get both girls out of these wet clothes before hypothermia set in. If it hadn't already.

CHAPTER FOUR

Noel handed the blanket back to the paramedic. "Thanks for this."

"Thank you guys for what you did." The tall human female with dark brown skin tucked the blanket under her arm. "You sure you don't want to hitch a ride to the hospital? Even just stop by to be checked out?" Concern rolled off her in waves.

Noel glanced up at Nathan, who shook his head. Smiling, she looked back at the woman who was just trying to do her job. Of course she would want them to go to the hospital, but there was no need. Even their busted-up knuckles were already healed. "We're good, I promise. I might call for an update though."

"Please do. I think those girls are going to be okay." She nodded once at Sheriff Parker McIntyre, who was fast approaching, before she headed around to the front of the ambulance. The one transporting the girls to the local hospital had left a while ago.

Thankfully some very nice citizens of Fontana had scrounged up some dry clothes for her and Nathan. Though considering some of the looks he'd gotten, a lot of women in town were sad to see all that bare skin covered up. Nathan picked up their bag of wet clothes and she could tell he was ready to go. She was too, but wanted to talk to Parker first.

Parker pulled her into a hug as soon as he reached them, and to Noel's surprise, Nathan let out the barest hint of a growl.

Surprise ricocheting through her, she stepped back. "What are you doing here?" She'd asked one of the paramedics and learned Parker was off tonight, so he wasn't wearing a uniform.

"I was having dinner downtown when I got the news. Why aren't you two at the hospital?" he demanded, looking between her and Nathan, frustration on his face.

"Because we're fine." Nathan's voice was icier than the snow on the ground.

Noel nudged him with her elbow as she smiled at Parker. The male was December's brother and while he'd gotten off to a rocky start with their pack, now he was family. As well as a good friend to the pack.

"You know how stubborn we shifters can be," she said as Nathan placed a possessive hand on the back of her neck. *Okay, then.* She couldn't deny how much she like it.

Parker nodded, his expression annoyed. "Yes, I do. Thank you for what you did. If it hadn't been for your quick thinking…" He shook his head before holding out a hand to Nathan—who thankfully took it—and then Noel.

"Are you coming by the ranch for Christmas?" she asked.

"Yeah, got something really good for Ellie." The joy on his face was unmistakable as he talked about his niece and Noel was glad that whatever tension had once been between him and his sister was water under the bridge. "Look, you guys need a ride home or anything?"

"We're good," Nathan said, his voice normal this time. "But thanks."

"All right. I'll see you around, then." Instead of hugging her again, like she'd expected, he just nodded and headed off.

Nathan slid an arm around her shoulders and she leaned into him, inhaled his dark scent. Tonight had been terrifying and eye-opening. For the past year she'd been a shadow of her former self. What had almost happened to those little girls could have happened to anyone.

She might be a shifter with a longer life span but she wasn't immortal. "I bet those kids get anything they want for Christmas this year," she murmured, a shiver racking her body that had nothing to do with the cold. What if she and Nathan hadn't been here tonight? And what if someone hadn't gotten to the girls in time? That family would be mourning right now.

"No kidding." His grip was tight as they strode down the sidewalk back to downtown. Most of the place had cleared out an hour ago, after the first ambulance had left.

The rest of the walk to Main Street they were quiet, though there were still shoppers and diners milling around downtown.

It gave her too much time to think, to realize what a coward she was being. She still needed to talk to someone about her grief, that much she knew. And she still felt like a mess—and figured that Nathan deserved someone a lot more put together than her.

But...he wanted *her*. And God help her, she wanted him. She hoped he'd be patient with her as she tried to get her shit together.

"Nathan," she whispered as they reached his truck, pausing as a giggling teenage couple passed them holding hands. Once they were gone no one else was near them on the sidewalk. She took a deep breath, ready to tell him...she wasn't even sure what. No words formed when she saw that deep hunger in his bright green eyes.

Talking could be overrated anyway.

Tugging on the long-sleeved T-shirt someone had given him, she yanked him down to her. His mouth met hers in a hard, hungry clash of lips and tongue that left her breathless and wanting way more when he pulled back.

His eyes glittered, a soft growl building in his throat as he leaned down to nip at her lips, softer this time. Sweeter.

He tasted just like she remembered. All spicy, sexy masculinity. Her nipples tightened against her bra as he slid his free arm around her back, pulled her close to him. She heard the bag drop to the sidewalk before his other hand slid to her nape, his fingers flexing possessively.

A riot of emotions ricocheted through her, but mainly she just felt happy to be alive. *He* made her feel alive.

Much too soon, he pulled back again.

Disappointment slid through her, but they were on Main Street. Making out by his truck like teenagers wasn't exactly appropriate. At the moment she didn't really care though.

"I'm still a mess, Nathan." She cleared her throat. "I don't know what I can offer you right now." It would be unfair of her to pretend otherwise.

Gently, he took her face in his hands, making her breath catch in her throat. "I know what it's like to lose people. Life's too short to close yourself off forever."

"I know," she whispered.

"However long it takes you to be ready for us, I'll wait. I just want to spend time with you—and only you."

His words shattered through her, breaking down more of the wall she'd erected around herself. She hadn't scented another female on him so she figured she understood what he meant about only her.

Nodding, she lifted up on her tiptoes and brushed her lips over his. "Then let's spend some time together this week," she murmured as she pulled back.

"You want to help me decorate my Christmas tree?"

She was surprised he hadn't done that yet, but nodded. It was weird to think that just this morning she was cursing the holiday season, when now the thought of doing something Christmas-related with Nathan was...kind of perfect.

Deep down she was terrified that if she let him in, got too close, he'd be ripped away from her too. But screw that—he could be ripped away from her whether she got too close or not.

She'd already lost too many people, and the thought of not getting to know Nathan better, not finding out what they could have, was scarier than any of her fears.

* * *

Erin leaned her head back against the headrest of the SUV, ready to get back to the ranch and jump her mate, Noah. Their last Council job had been stupidly easy but the last few months had been exhausting overall. She was ready for home cooking and to see her packmates.

Noah glanced at her. "We're almost done with this jackass, then we'll be home."

"Hey, I can hear you," their prisoner grumbled from the backseat. The sixteen-year-old cub, who thought he was a full-grown Alpha for some insane reason, had decided to rip off a pack neighboring his own, then go on the run once his own Alpha—also his father—found out.

"What were you thinking, kid?" she muttered as Noah steered through downtown Fontana. Everywhere she looked sparkled with the holiday spirit. It soothed every part of her. Christmas was one of her favorite times of year.

The kid wasn't from here, but his father was meeting them nearby to pick up his errant boy. This was literally the easiest job she'd ever been tasked by The Council. Her only instructions had been to not hurt the cub. Considering how unskilled and nonviolent he was, he hadn't posed a threat to them, so not a problem. Usually her jobs consisted of taking down violent offenders who refused to follow human or pack law.

"I...wanted to impress a female," he muttered. "She's three years older than me and hot. I knew she'd be home for the holidays from college."

Erin stifled a laugh. "So you thought stealing from a neighboring pack would impress her?"

"She once dated the dude I stole from. He was a jerk to her, made her cry when they broke up."

Erin glanced at Noah, raised her eyebrows. What kind of screwed-up teenage logic was that? Noah just shrugged, his own lips twitching.

"Holy crap." She pointed out the window as they passed two of their packmates. "That's Noel and Nathan making out."

Her mate shook his head. "About time he made his move."

"Right? I never thought he'd go after her." She blinked as they continued past the two and wondered when the heck things between them had changed. She was clearly out of the loop on pack gossip.

"Maybe you two could just let me go, say I escaped," the kid said, hope in his voice.

Erin snorted. "You gotta pay for your crimes, Gavin. Besides, no one's gonna believe you escaped from me." Not arrogance, just the truth.

"Yeah, I know. My dad's gonna have me locked down for probably a year."

"And you deserve worse. Jeez." She turned in her seat, eyed the handsome blond-haired, blue-eyed cub who looked like he'd be at home on a surfboard. "If you want to impress a female, learn to do it in a different way. Stand out from the crowd. Don't be the jackass showoff. And don't call her 'hot.' It makes you sound like a cub. You think a woman likes that?"

His lips pulled into a thin line, but he shook his head. Then, "How'd he win you over?" He jerked his chin in Noah's direction, but kept his gaze on Erin.

"By treating me like an equal, by respecting my strength and by being himself." And by loving all of her, even the broken parts. There was no one in the world for her but her Noah. If something happened to him, she knew she'd follow him into the afterlife.

She wouldn't be able to live without him. And she was okay with that.

Frowning thoughtfully, the kid nodded as Noah steered into a parking lot.

Erin turned back in her seat. "Give me a sec before getting the kid out," she murmured. She wanted to talk to the Alpha first.

Noah nodded.

To her surprise, it was just a single male waiting for them. "What's the girl's name, anyway?" she asked Gavin.

"Paisley." His voice was full of worship.

Shaking her head, she got out when Noah parked two spots over and strode to meet Kenneth McAndrews. The male was an older version of his son, with the same California-surfer-type good looks.

"My boy's okay?" Subtle power rolled off the Alpha as he crossed his arms over his broad chest.

"He's fine. Look, it's not my business, but go easy on him if you can. He did it to impress—"

"Paisley, I know. He's been in love with her since he was ten." His father shook his head, a smile tugging at his lips. "I'm just glad you found him. He'll be punished but...it's Christmas."

Relief flooded her. The cub might be stupid and immature but heck, he was a *cub*. They were supposed to be like that in their teenage years. This job had been more a favor to The Council anyway since McAndrews was apparently friends with one of the Council members.

Erin turned, nodded at Noah through the window. She couldn't see past the tint but knew he saw her.

A moment later Noah tugged Gavin out, released the wrist restraints and walked the kid around the front of SUV toward them, his hand on the back of Gavin's neck.

The kid looked at his feet, clearly ashamed as he approached his father. The big male didn't pause, just tugged Gavin into his arms, crushing him in a hug. "Don't ever run away again." Emotion clogged his voice as he held his son. "Your mom and I were worried sick about you."

"I'm sorry, Dad." Regret laced his words as he stepped back. "I panicked and just...didn't think."

Erin nodded at her mate. It was time for them to get out of there. They'd done their job and she was ready to get home. She knew the Alpha was just concerned about his kid and they didn't need to stay for the family reunion.

"Hey, wait, uh, please." Gavin pulled his cell phone out of his pocket. "I know you think I'm a stupid kid, but would you take a selfie with me?"

She blinked, and next to her Noah snickered under his breath.

"Come on," Gavin continued. "Paisley's a big fan of yours. If I get a picture with the newest enforcer? That'll impress her for sure!"

Behind the kid his father sighed and rubbed an exhausted hand over his face.

"Fine, but I'm not smiling," she said, sidling up next to the kid. "So let's get this over with." She couldn't believe she was taking a selfie with one of her captures, but this kid was starting to grow on her.

After he'd taken the picture, he grinned. "You think I could touch one of your blades?"

She lifted an eyebrow, not bothering to respond.

"Yeah, okay, it was a long shot." Smiling, he held out a hand. "You look totally badass in the picture. Thanks for taking it. And Merry Christmas."

Shaking his hand, she half-smiled at Gavin and hoped that one day he won his female over. "Merry Christmas, kid."

Noah burst into full-on laughter once they were alone in the SUV and on the road. "Oh my God, you took a selfie!" His laughter filled the enclosed space, soothed every part of her.

"What was I supposed to do, say no to that puppy dog face?" She smothered a smile, and mock-glared at her mate.

"I'm pretty sure I love you even more now." He leaned over after stopping at a red light, brushed his lips over hers. "Would you mind if we make some stops before we head back to the ranch? I need to grab a couple more things for the cubs."

"I do too." Christmas was fast approaching and she'd barely bought anything. They were doing a gift exchange during the big pack Christmas Eve party, but everyone got stuff for the cubs. "Gah, they're gone," she said as they drove past the place where Noel and Nathan had been kissing.

Noah snorted. "You expected them to still be going at it on the side of the street?"

Erin just shrugged and pointed to a car pulling out of a curbside spot. "Grab it!"

"I love you, mate of mine, but no backseat driving." His voice was dry as he pulled into the spot he'd seen without her help.

"I can't help it. I miss my baby."

"Some days I think I should be jealous of your Challenger."

Laughing, she got out of the SUV, her boots crunching over some of the icy slush on the road before she met him on the sidewalk. "If it ever came down to it, I'd choose you over my car." She might be a teeny bit obsessed with her cherry red Challenger.

He wrapped his arm around her shoulders, pulled her close as they headed down the sidewalk. "That's good to know—"

She gasped when they reached the front window of December's Book Nook and saw the display. "I'm going to kill someone." She marched inside before her mate could say anything, ignoring the little jingle of the bell overhead.

When she saw Gloria coming out from one of the aisles, a handful of books in her hand, she lost some of her steam. She couldn't very well yell at a beta pack member. It would be like picking on a puppy. "Hey, Gloria."

The dark-haired female gave her a warm smile. "Hey, guys. I thought you were out of town. What's—oh, did you see the new display?" She gave a little wince. "They just came in today."

"Take them down," she snapped out before she could stop herself.

"I can't—unless you want to buy them all." Gloria struggled to hide a smile, failed miserably. "I've already sold a dozen."

Noah slung an arm around Erin's shoulders, nuzzled the top of her head. "They look good."

She glared at him before turning to look at the big display of Erin Flynn action figures. It was so beyond ridiculous she didn't even know what to do. She really wanted to scream at the sight of them and slice them up with her blades until they were just bits of plastic on the ground.

Eight months ago she'd killed some vampires who been on a rampage of destruction. Unfortunately, someone had caught the kills on their cell phone and the video had gone viral in hours. She hadn't been in trouble. No, she'd been hailed a hero, a defender of humans—and The Council ate that shit up. Her friend Kat had joked that they'd soon come out with action figures of her—which they had, as of a month ago. It was why the kid Gavin had known who she was. Apparently, she had an actual fan club. So fucking stupid.

Now there was a whole display of little Erin figures in the front window of December's bookstore. This was beyond embarrassing.

"You should be proud." Noah's voice was sincere as he tugged her close. "Shifter females need someone to look up to."

She eyed him warily. "And The Council chose me?"

"No, your badass skills got you chosen." Grinning, he crushed his mouth to hers, the need and hunger thrumming through him a palpable thing she swore she could feel in her bones.

We need to get out of here now, she said along their telepathic bondmate link.

Breathing erratically, he pulled back, his wolf in his eyes, and simply nodded.

Once they were outside she realized they hadn't even said goodbye to Gloria. They'd just run out of there.

Oh well, it was better than turning into complete animals in the middle of the bookstore. For how she felt, she wanted to feel her mate filling her, claiming her and making her generally crazy as soon as possible. They might not even make it back to their house this time. The SUV would work just as well as anyplace, as far as she was concerned.

Considering the thick scent of lust rolling off her sexy-as-sin mate, she was pretty sure he'd be on board with that too.

CHAPTER FIVE

Gloria was thinking about closing up December's Book Nook when Kat and Jayce walked in holding hands. "Hey, you just missed Erin and Noah." Erin was an enforcer, just like Jayce.

Gloria didn't know the male well, and the truth was, she didn't want to. He was a bit scary, but he was friends with the male she'd been seeing the last month—the very frustrating vampire who'd been acting strange and distant for the last three days.

Gloria wished Niko would just open up to her, but she couldn't make him. And if he didn't want to be in a relationship anymore, then she wished he'd just tell her. He hadn't been around, had told her he'd been busy working—and she would understand if that was the truth. But something about his tone and attitude made her think he hadn't been exactly honest with her.

Not that it would be easy to walk away. No, it would shred her heart apart, but she couldn't deal with this not knowing what was going on between the two of them. As a beta she needed affection and to know she was important. It was how she was wired. So this three days of weirdness between them had her all twisted up inside.

"Did she see the display?" Kat asked, her pale blue eyes glowing with glee. The tall female who'd once been human had been turned to a shifter to save her life after a horrific near-death experience. She was one of the most beautiful females Gloria had ever met. She looked as if she should be on a movie screen. Lean, leggy and ultra-confident. If they weren't friends, she might be a little intimidated by Kat.

"Yeah. Didn't seem too happy about it either." December had warned Gloria that Erin would probably hate them, but The Council apparently wanted the pack to sell them, so...it was happening. And they'd been a pretty big seller so far today. A lot of human girls wanted them. Gloria couldn't blame them after seeing the video of Erin in action. She'd looked just like a superhero from the movies, all liquid, lethal grace as she'd killed those vamps with incredible ease.

Kat's grin widened. "I'll take all of them. Including the ones you have in the back."

She blinked. "That's like almost two hundred."

"Perfect!"

Jayce gave Kat a wry look. "I'm afraid to even ask, but why do you want all the figurines?"

"You'll see." Her lips curved up mischievously as she gave him a sideways glance. "Oh, we need to stop by a craft store after this too."

"I can grab the boxes from the back, then?" Gloria asked, looking between the two of them, unsure if they were actually taking the entire stock.

"Yes, please," Kat said, pulling her wallet from her purse.

Jayce just gave her a dark look and pulled out his own. "I've got this."

Gloria figured that she'd find out soon enough what Kat planned to do with all of the figures. Once the couple was gone, burdened down by multiple boxes, Gloria ran the end-of-the-day reports and closed up shop.

She probably could have stayed another hour but she was exhausted, and December had told her she could close early if she wanted.

Glad she didn't have to do a bank deposit tonight, she tucked the store keys into her pocket and pulled the belt of her peacoat tighter around her. The chill in the air was crisp and made her wolf side happy. She preferred the cold over the heat any day.

Passing happy couples and families as she strolled down the sidewalk, she tried to keep her mind off Niko, but it was impossible. She'd met the sexy vampire a month ago and it was as if some part of her she hadn't even realized existed had woken up.

They'd met and she'd been stunned speechless by the connection between them. He had been too, thankfully.

The last three days, however, he'd been acting strange. He hadn't even been able to stay during the days at her place and had been cagey when she asked why. Which wasn't like the male she thought she knew.

She didn't want to put chains on him, but something just felt weird and she'd learned not to ignore her instinct. For the most part, no shifter ignored that intrinsic part of themselves.

Instead of going back to the ranch she decided to go see the huge Christmas tree in one of the local parks. Everyone from Fontana was allowed to donate an ornament, which usually made for an over-decorated tree. But she loved it. Loved everything about where she lived.

Even if she ached to get away sometimes. Her sister Natalia had been going on adventures lately, working with her new mate Aldric, and even with the enforcer, Jayce, on different missions. It was hard not to feel a little left behind.

The truth was, though, she didn't want to go bounty hunting. She was more peaceful and submissive by nature, but...that didn't mean she wouldn't love to travel. Unfortunately, her former pack Alpha had been so damn strict with everyone, not just the females. Now she wanted to spread her wings, to see more of the world. Sometimes she felt like it was passing her by. Especially after losing so many of her packmates, cousins and her parents to violence.

A few days ago she and Niko had started talking about planning a trip to New Zealand in the new year—right before he pretty much ghosted on her. Had she been wrong about him? About them?

When she turned the corner onto a side street that would take her to the park, she frowned when she spotted Niko's car parked along the curb. A small sheet of snow covered the hood, telling her it had been there a little while at least. Nearing it, she saw that it was in front of a little café that was closed.

He'd told her he had work stuff tonight. An uncomfortable sensation twisted inside her, but she shoved it back. She trusted Niko. He'd given her no reason not to. The male had a lot of businesses and conducted most things online. But maybe he'd had a meeting in town.

Seemed kind of late for one, but— She stopped walking when he stepped out the café with a tall blonde woman wearing five-inch knee-high boots and a body-hugging sweater dress. Her coat was draped over her arm.

"I apologize for keeping you so long," he said to the woman, who was locking up. His eyes widened when he saw Gloria standing on the sidewalk.

The woman gave a throaty laugh and said something to him, but Gloria didn't hear her response. Didn't actually care what it was.

Awkwardness invaded her as he stared at her like a deer caught in headlights. Was he...with this woman? As a beta shifter she wasn't confrontational. Not even close. Some betas were, but she was more passive in every sense. She hated conflict, and right about now she wanted to be anywhere but here.

Erin or Kat would probably walk straight up to him and ask what the hell he was doing. Or at least keep their cool.

Gloria's instinct was to simply flee, however. Which was stupid. She knew that. But Niko looked guilty as hell and she didn't want some uncomfortable confrontation with him in front of some random female he was hooking up with.

Her canines descended at that thought. Turning away, she'd taken two steps down the sidewalk when Niko was all of a sudden standing in front of her in a blur of motion.

"What are you doing here?" His dark eyes had a soft glow to them as he reached for her, took one of her hands in his.

She could hear the female coming down the walkway toward them, ignored her. "I closed the bookstore up early and wanted to go see the big Christmas tree in the park. What are you doing here?" There was a bite to her words she couldn't hide.

Before he could respond the human reached them. "You must be Gloria."

She turned to the woman, surprised she knew her name. "Yes."

"You're a lucky lady," she said, smiling warmly before winking at Niko. "I'll see you tomorrow to finish everything up. Have a good night." She was gone in a blur of clicking heels and slightly cloying perfume as she crossed the street toward a small, gated parking lot.

Gloria turned back to Niko, who definitely looked guilty. "Who is that woman?"

"I..." He raked a hand through his midnight black hair.

"If you want to end things, just tell me." She pulled her hand back, wrapped her arms around herself.

His dark eyes widened. "What? No! I'd wanted it to be a surprise for Christmas. That was Angela. She's, well, she's a real estate agent, among other things."

She frowned. "One who runs a café?

"Oh, no. Her sister owns that place. She let us close up late so we could go over... Which isn't the point. She's a Realtor and was recommended to me by a friend as being reliable. I've planned a yearlong trip for us—if you want—and bought some new places all over the world. I can't trust where I sleep to hotels, so I had to get all the arrangements set up before I surprised you."

She blinked, letting her arms fall from around her as his words settled in. "You planned a trip for us?"

He nodded, settling his big hands on her hips. "When you started talking about going to New Zealand I realized you wanted to see more of the world."

She placed her hands on his chest, dug her fingers into his shirt. Yes, this man understood her well. Relief swelled inside her that he didn't want to end things.

"I wanted everything to be perfect," he said, his voice raspier than normal. He'd had his throat cut before he'd been turned into a vampire, and after the transition it hadn't changed.

"I feel like an idiot. You've been so distant the last couple days and then I saw you with that woman and I thought..." Her cheeks heated as she looked at him. "Wait, you *bought* homes for us to stay in?" She couldn't have heard *that* right. She knew the male had money but...that was crazy.

Now he flushed, and considering he was a five-hundred-year-old vampire, it was adorable. "Some I already own, but yes. I wanted to make certain I'd be safe in every residence and that you'd be protected during the day."

"You're a wonderful, wonderful man, Nikolai. Thank you for such an amazing gift. I can't even wrap my head around a trip like this." She rose on her tiptoes and touched her lips to his. His body temperature was slightly cooler than hers and she loved the contrast. She'd never imagined she'd end up with a vampire, but now she couldn't imagine being with anyone but this male.

He growled softly. "Love it when you say my full name."

She loved everything about the male. "You want to go see the big Christmas tree with me?" she whispered.

Lightly nipping her bottom lip, he let out a growl, which could have been a yes or no. When he slid an arm around her shoulders and led her in that direction, she figured it was a yes.

"A whole year?" she asked, leaning her head against his shoulder as they rounded the next corner. All the poles lining the street were strung with bright twinkly lights.

"If that's okay with you. I know you haven't been many places and I want to show you everything." Heat and something else laced his voice. He was ancient compared to her, so worldly and experienced. She couldn't wait to see the world with him.

"It's more than okay. Thank you for this gift." It was like the male was in her head. Even if he hadn't broached the subject of mating, she knew he adored her, and he'd told her he loved her. And she loved him. She'd realized it about a week into their relationship, which felt impossibly soon. But again, as a shifter, she'd never doubted her instinct. Wasn't going to start now.

She scented roasted chestnuts from a vendor a street over and just a hint of hot cocoa in the air, probably from the same vendor, as they crossed the final street toward the park. Her boots thudded softly along the sidewalk but Niko was stealth personified.

She was surprised that no one was at the huge tree when they reached it, but it was getting kind of late. It towered about eighteen feet into the air, ringed with green, red and white lights and mismatched ornaments. A soft blanket of snow covered everything, even layering some of the branches.

"Gloria." Niko's voice was a low rumble.

When she turned in his arms, he dropped his hold and went down on one knee.

It took her a moment to realize what he was doing until he pulled out a small blue box. He opened it to reveal a sparkly diamond ring. Princess cut and huge. "No matter what you say—"

"Yes!" she threw her arms around him, and if he wasn't ridiculously strong and ancient she'd have probably tackled him to the ground.

A low chuckle rumbled in his chest. "I had a whole speech prepared about how I still value human traditions from my era."

Grinning and feeling foolish as they both knelt by the twinkling tree in the snow, she said, "Finish it, then."

His mouth curved up slightly. "I thought I might have to convince you."

She blinked. How could this male ever doubt how much she loved him? "Seriously?"

"I never thought I'd meet anyone like you. When I saw you in Connor's living room it was like…" He shook his head, his expression a little awed.

"I know." She'd felt it too. Like lightning striking.

"I want to mate as well as marry. In case that wasn't clear. I want everything from you. I was worried about going too fast but before this trip, before we start our lives together, I want the whole world to know you're mine. Humans and supernaturals."

Those were words she'd needed to hear, on every level. Throat tight with emotion, she wrapped her arms around his neck. "Tonight. We mate tonight." She'd imagined it for so long.

His dark eyes glinted with lust, the scent of him dark and spicy. "I love it when you get bossy," he murmured.

"And I love you."

He growled low in his throat, sounding more shifter than vampire. "I love you too." Scooping her in his arms, he lifted them in the air, something they'd only done once before. Not many vampires could fly, but he was one of the few.

She let out a short gasp as the cold air rushed over them. Right now she figured they were headed back to wherever he was staying. And they were most definitely going to make things permanent tonight, in the most intimate way possible. Marriage was fine with her, but bonding was what her wolf craved.

She wanted forever with her vampire.

* * *

Aldric paused in the doorway of the kitchen, watching as his mate did a fist pump into the air. "What's that for?"

Natalia swiveled in her chair at the center island, her dark ponytail swinging back, and held up her cell phone. "Gloria's not coming home tonight."

He grinned, stepped closer to his new mate. If Gloria wasn't coming home, it meant they were about to get naked. They were moving out soon, but their new home wasn't even close to being ready yet. The ranch had seen a lot of new construction lately, including their home, which was basically a frame right now.

"Niko made his move, finally. Told her about the trip he's been planning. They leave after Christmas." Sadness flickered in her dark eyes for a moment. "I'm bummed she'll be gone for so long but maybe we can plan a trip to meet up with them somewhere."

He set his hands on the counter on either side of her, caging her in as she fully turned to him.

"I'm glad for your sister," he murmured, his gaze on her mouth. "But I'm really glad for us right now."

"Why's that?" She spread her legs, a wicked grin on her face as he stepped closer.

He placed his palms on her thighs, slid them up higher and higher until his thumbs touched her covered mound. Oh yeah, these jeans were about to be gone. "Because I plan to have you naked in—"

Knock, knock, knock.

Aldric gritted his teeth. "I'm going to kill whoever's out there. Our door is locked for a reason."

His sweet mate just brushed her lips against his and slid out of the chair, laughing as she ducked under his arm. "I'll open it so you don't bite off the head of whoever it is."

Sighing, he followed her to the front door. He'd recently joined the Armstrong-Cordona pack, after mating with Natalia, a female he couldn't live without. The last pack he'd been part of hundreds of years ago had been much smaller by comparison, and composed of mostly his immediately family. Now he found they were always bombarded by someone. And he was often working patrols, helping to make sure that pack land was secured from anyone with malicious intent or curious humans, so he didn't get nearly as much time with his mate as he wanted.

He scented Kat, his brother's mate, before Natalia even opened the door.

The female had a big grin on her face as she held out a small brown bag. "Make sure you hang these on your tree."

Natalia peered into the bag, grinned, then handed it to Aldric. Looking inside, he saw that someone, likely Kat, had turned the new Erin action figures into Christmas ornaments.

"Where'd you get these?" Natalia asked, leaning against the doorframe. Kat had a big canvas bag filled with other smaller brown paper bags just like this one.

"Bought them from December's place and added the hooks myself. They're going to look awesome on everyone's trees."

"She hates these things."

Kat snorted. "I know, but it's awesome and I like making her crazy."

"Do you also like getting killed?" Natalia asked dryly.

"Erin's gotta catch me first." She grinned mischievously and dashed off the porch. "I'll catch y'all later. I've got more deliveries to make. And I better see those on your tree next time I'm here."

Chuckling, Natalia shut the door and plucked the bag from Aldric's hand. "Let's put these on now."

"I can think of something better we could be doing." He followed her into the living room, soaked in all the Christmas decorations. Since it was his first real Christmas in centuries, Natalia had gone all-out and was making a huge deal over the holiday.

He'd told her she didn't need to, but deep down, he was glad she loved him enough to do this. The only thing he needed in his life was her, but spending their first Christmas together like this...reminded him how damn lucky he was to have her.

"Soon, I promise." She hooked one of the ornaments onto the tree and handed the bag to Aldric. "Maybe this will become a new tradition. Erin ornaments on all our trees."

Laughing at the ridiculousness of the situation, he took a handful of the figures and added them to the tree as well.

He couldn't believe how much his life had changed since he'd met Natalia. He'd gone from being a lonely, solitary wolf with nothing to live for, to having every-thing he could have ever wanted. A family, a pack, and her.

The female he loved more than anything. The female he'd be spending the rest of his life with, would have a family with eventually. He was never letting her go.

CHAPTER SIX

Energy and excitement hummed through Noel as she walked across the yard to the guys' cabin. She'd wanted to help Nathan decorate his tree yesterday but the psychologist December recommended had been able to work her in, so she'd jumped at the chance to take the appointment.

She knew she had a way to go in emotional healing, but making the first step in getting help made her feel as if she could get through everything, could start to get a handle on her life again.

When she reached the front door, it swung open before she'd knocked. Nathan stood there as if he'd been waiting for her, all ridiculously sexy as he gave her a slow smile. His green eyes darkened and that spicy scent of his heat filled the air, wrapping around her. Her stomach filled with butterflies at the mere sight and scent of him.

"Hey." She did a mental fist pump, glad she'd managed to get a word out when she could just stare at the sexy male forever. After how sweet he'd been on Wednesday, clearly not wanting to push her into anything too soon, she had no doubt what a good male he was. And...he was the type of male she could see herself with long-term. Not even just the type of male. *He* was who she could see herself with and it scared her a little.

"Hey, yourself," he murmured. "Thanks for coming over. I found a couple bins marked as ornaments in one of the closets, figured we could use them." He stepped back to let her in and she finally realized he was wearing a Star Wars T-shirt. Chewbacca was on the front wearing a Santa hat.

Laughing, she slid her coat off and handed it to him. His gaze immediately landed on her own T-shirt—Darth Vader wearing an ugly Christmas sweater. She'd found it in her closet this morning. It had belonged to Carmen and wearing it made her feel closer to her sister.

"So we're both nerds," he said, taking her coat.

"I think you mean we're both awesome." She left her boots by the door, hating how much height she lost when she took them off. "But confession time— I've never seen all the movies. This was Carmen's."

His eyebrows raised. "I think I see a movie marathon in our future."

Her belly did a flip-flop at the way he said 'our.' Yeah, she could get on board with that. "I'll bring the popcorn."

His gaze went heated again but he quickly turned and motioned to the main living area and bare Christmas tree in one corner. It hadn't been there Wednesday when she'd come by so he must have just put it up. The scent of pine needles teased the air. A half-eaten string of popcorn fell haphazardly from the tree.

"What happened to your popcorn?"

"Pretty sure Vivian got in here and ate it. Well, her or Lucas."

Noel snorted. "My money's on Viv." She lived with the adorable eleven-year-old jaguar cub, and to say she was mischievous was the understatement of the century.

"No kidding... I've, uh, never really decorated a tree before." He sounded almost sheepish as he admitted it.

"Really? Not even as a cub?" She knelt down next to one of the plastic containers marked 'ornaments' and recognized her mother's handwriting. Seeing it was a punch to her chest. Her pack had used two of the closets in this cabin as storage before the males from Connor's group moved in. Most of the stuff was still in there.

"Nah, my parents didn't celebrate anything really. They were good parents, but more in touch with their wolf side. Didn't care much about integrating with humans or traditions."

"Where'd you guys live before..." She didn't want to finish the thought, didn't want to say the words and cause him any pain. She looked up as he knelt next to her, opened another container.

"All over, but we were in Montana when they were killed. I roamed for a while afterward, tried out a couple different packs, then went solo until I met Connor and Liam."

"I'm glad you met them." As soon as the words were out, she realized how true they were. She might have been blind to him the last year, but looking at huge, muscled Nathan in his silly T-shirt, she was very glad he'd joined their pack. Was very glad he was in her life.

"Me too." His voice dropped an octave as he carefully watched her. He cleared his throat. "I don't know if there will ever be an appropriate time to say this so…I'm just throwing it out there. I haven't been with anyone since our kisses a year ago. I haven't wanted to. Just thought you might want to know."

Holy… Talk about a subject change. She wasn't sure how to respond to that. The truth was, she *had* wondered about it. He was a sexy, alpha shifter who would have no problem finding female company. Wednesday at the skating rink she'd noticed at least a dozen females checking him out, and the most insecure part of her had wondered how many women he'd been with since her. Had hated how jealous it made her. It didn't matter that she had no right to be jealous. "I'm glad," she rasped out.

The reason behind what he'd admitted wasn't lost on her either. But she wasn't ready to think about that. Not yet. It was too huge.

Looking away under his intense scrutiny because that was a conversation path she wasn't sure she wanted to travel down, she popped open the lid of the container closest to her. "These bad boys are true art, my friend." She held up two snowflakes made from twigs that had been decorated with buttons, twine and a whole lot of glitter. Most of the glitter was gone now. Green stained her fingers as she set them on the coffee table next to her.

"I can see that." His oh-so-sexy mouth kicked up at the corners. "You make them?"

"Yeah. Ana, Carmen and me, when we were cubs. I can't believe we still have these." She shifted the snowflakes to the side and found a bundle of wreaths made from small birch discs and tiny red plastic berries—and of course more glitter. "We had a theme every year. My mom set everything up and we, as well as my younger cousins, all got together and made ornaments. These look a little fragile though... I'm not sure if we should use them."

She looked up at him, the flood of memories bringing back a feeling of warmth. Her Alpha might have been hard to live with but they sure had a lot of good memories.

"Would you want to go into town with me and hit up the craft store? You can make your very own ornaments." Part of her wanted him to experience that anyway. To form new, happy memories he could treasure for years to come. Some intrinsic part of her needed to do this for him. Sure, it was a little nerdy, and she might have been cursing Christmas this year, but she cherished all the holiday memories she'd had over the decades.

"I'll go anywhere with you." Something about the way he said it, the drop in his tone, sent out a frisson of awareness to her nerve endings.

She cleared her throat. "After we decorate, maybe we can watch one of the Star Wars movies?" She wanted to do more than just watch a movie. A replay of one of their kisses—and maybe more—was definitely in order.

Taking her hand, he pulled her to her feet as he stood. "Perfect."

After they put on their boots, he took her hand again. And as he grabbed their coats from the rack by the door, she noticed he still held on tight, as if he couldn't stop touching her. And she didn't pull away.

When they stepped outside onto the porch, she was sad when he let go to help her into her coat. But as soon as it was on, he took her hand in his again. Oh yeah, he was making a statement to anyone who saw them. Though it was icy outside with a forecast of more snow that afternoon, neither of them wore gloves.

She was glad to have that skin-to-skin contact, however small it was.

"Want to take my truck?"

"Yeah." Their boots crunched over the snow and iced-over grass as they headed to the huge shed everyone parked in. "How'd you get out of work today?"

"Switched days with Jacob." One of the only other single male wolves.

"That was nice of him." Noel made a mental note to bake the other male cookies. Or...ask Ana to, anyway. "So, I saw that doctor yesterday." She felt weird talking about visiting a psychologist but she really wanted Nathan to know.

He squeezed her hand once before wrapping an arm around her shoulders. "How'd it go?"

God, how had she been so blind to him this last year? She leaned into him, soaked up all that strength and warmth. "Really good. A little strange at first just talking, but...the guy's a shifter and really down to earth. And he's lost people too."

"He told you that?"

"Sorta, yeah. He didn't say who, or anything, but it came up organically when I snapped at him, asking if he'd ever lost anyone. I...don't know why I thought he wouldn't have. It was such a stupid, arrogant question. God, every shifter I know has lost someone. If not to violence, then their human friends to old age."

"I still think about my younger brother. Think about how things might have been different if I'd been there that day."

He'd told Noel that his brother had been sixteen, had looked up to him. She squeezed his waist, holding him tighter. "You might not be here right now if you had." That thought shredded her up inside.

"I know." He kissed the top of her head as they reached his truck, and instead of opening the passenger door he pressed her against it and covered her mouth with his.

She hadn't been expecting it, especially not the possessive hunger that sparked inside her. The second their lips touched, she arched into him, a wildfire of need spreading through her.

His kiss wasn't soft or sweet, but demanding and sensual. She clutched onto his shoulders, her heartbeat out of control as he slid a hand behind her head, holding her in place.

She didn't want to be anywhere else.

She moaned into his mouth, digging her fingers into his shoulders, her claws peeking out a fraction. She felt bad until he groaned.

"Oh, yeah," he murmured against her mouth, grinding his hips against hers. His erection was hard and unmistakable and she really, really wanted to see and touch his cock for herself. She had almost no experience with males, thanks to the previous structure of their pack's dynamics.

Tasting him like this made her remember exactly how combustible things had been between them a year ago. Her grief was the only thing that could have doused what they'd started to explore with each other.

It was truly like she'd come alive again and she wanted everything Nathan had to offer.

The sound of someone clearing their throat made her pull back, but only a fraction. She scented someone familiar and it took a long few seconds for her to recognize her packmate Aiden.

His longish blond hair was pulled back in a rubber band but he scrubbed a hand over the top of his head.

"I hate interrupting, but uh, you're blocking me in, man. And I've got someplace to be."

Nathan made a low growling sound, but didn't respond as he placed a hand on the small of Noel's back and opened the passenger door.

Noel finally found her voice as she slid into the seat. "Hey, Aiden."

"Hey, shorty. Glad you're finally putting my man here out of his misery."

She blinked, surprised by his words, but before she could respond, Nathan shut the door. He was around the truck and in the driver's seat in seconds. She waved at Aiden, who just looked amused as Nathan tore out of the spot.

"What did he mean, put you out of your misery?" She was pretty sure she understood perfectly well, but wanted to be sure.

Nathan lifted a broad shoulder. "He knows how I feel about you—how I've felt the past year."

Guilt infused her at the muted pain in his voice. Others had clearly known how much he'd been into her. "I'm sorry I didn't realize how you felt then."

Frowning, he turned to look at her before steering through the main gate. "Don't ever apologize. You were dealing with a lot. I feel like I should apologize for not trying harder."

She scooted closer so she sat in the middle of the bench seat. "You don't need to be sorry either." He'd done nothing wrong. "I'm just glad we figured out that..." She swallowed hard, struggling with how to phrase it. "That we have a chance at something real."

"Me too." He placed a hand over hers as they made their way down the long, winding drive.

For the first time in ages she felt happy and hopeful about the future. One thing she knew for sure: she wanted Nathan in it.

* * *

Aiden tried to tamp down the riot of emotions inside him as he headed into town. By nature he was easygoing, took things in stride.

Except where the safety of his mate, Larissa, was concerned. Not that he was sure she was in danger. No, but she'd flat-out lied to him this morning. She'd carefully worded her answers to the point he knew she was lying without her coming out and saying it.

It was making him edgy, riling up his wolf in a way that was hard to control.

His beautiful bondmate who he thought he'd lost decades ago had been awoken from a long coma-like sleep mere months ago. A sleep that had severed their bonding link, as if she'd died, leading him to believe she truly had.

He'd never gotten over her though, never moved on. How could he move on from *her*?

Larissa Danesti, from one of the purest bloodborn vampire lines, a rare bloodborn daywalker. She was his world.

And she was keeping secrets from him.

If he hadn't lost her once, hadn't been shattered so badly all those years ago, her behavior the last couple days wouldn't affect him so much.

But the darkest part of him needed to see her with his own eyes right now. Something was driving him forward, so he'd done something that he felt guilty about— he'd used her phone to track her movements.

He glanced at his own phone, watching her location move deeper into downtown. She'd told him she was going shopping—which she had, according to one of the stops she'd made. But she hadn't been there long.

She'd left Main Street not long after and was now heading into a residential area. She didn't know anyone in Fontana other than shifters.

Not that he knew of.

Members of the Brethren had been hounding her to join them, however. He wondered if they were in town, had requested a meeting? He'd told her he would support whatever decision she made. It was too much to believe she would keep something like that from him, however.

He knew he was acting crazy right now, but his wolf wouldn't let him turn around, go back to the ranch and wait for his bondmate to return.

Her phone eventually stopped moving so he drove through the cheery, brightly decorated downtown of

Fontana before he found himself in a quiet neighborhood of historical homes. And in front of a three-story bed and breakfast, which her car was sitting outside of.

There were four other vehicles in the long driveway so he parked and headed up to the front door.

She was probably going to be pissed he'd followed her here, but he was pissed she'd lied. And an omission was lying as far as he was concerned. They didn't keep secrets from each other. Or he hadn't thought they did.

Testing their bondmate link, he said, *Hey, sweetheart, what are you doing?*

A few moments later she said, *Holiday stuff. Busy now, talk to you later.*

He frowned as he opened the front door, her brush-off making all his hackles rise. A little bell jingled overhead, announcing his presence.

In the foyer there was a credenza to the side with a guest sign-in book and a vase filled with two dozen fresh red roses.

Various voices and scents filled the air. There were three humans inside and another shifter. Well that was interesting. It wasn't someone from his pack and as far as he knew, no one had told his Alpha that they'd be in town. And all outside shifters had to announce their presence to Connor when they were in his territory.

He also smelled Larissa's dark forest scent. It called to him, pulled him in like an addict. He started for the stairs when a tiny human woman with a mass of curly gray hair and wearing a dress that looked a lot like what he thought Mrs. Claus would wear stepped through a swinging door.

She smiled warmly at him. "Hello, dear. We don't have any openings at the moment, but we should by the end of the week."

He smiled politely at her, cleared his throat. *Think, think.* "I just wanted to know if you had any brochures. I've heard a lot about this place." The lie rolled off his tongue with ease. "I thought I'd bring my wife here for a weekend getaway."

She smiled even more broadly and opened one of the credenza doors. "What a lovely idea." She pulled out a handful of brochures. "This one has everything you'll need to know about my home. But I've included some other brochures on local spas and fun things to do around here. I'm sure you already know about the ski lodges. We've got a great relationship with them and if you tell them you're staying here, they'll usually discount your ski rentals. And of course we're online so feel free to follow us on social media."

He nearly snorted. *He* wasn't on any social media. The humans could keep that shit for themselves. But he smiled. "This is wonderful, thank you."

"I—" She winced at the sound of glass breaking in a nearby room. The kitchen, if he had to guess. "Ah, excuse me for just a moment."

As soon as the swinging door closed behind her, he hurried up the stairs on quiet feet, following Larissa's scent and squashing his conscience that he was acting insane.

He knew he was. He just didn't give a shit.

Her dark forest scent led to a door on the end of the second-floor hallway. He knocked once and was almost surprised when it opened a moment later.

A pretty female shifter with blonde hair and dark brown eyes opened the door and just stared at him. Behind her he saw Larissa sitting on a tufted crimson chaise lounge by a window.

Her indigo blue eyes flashed with surprise, then distress. She jolted to her feet, her blue-black hair a waterfall over her shoulder. "What are you doing here?"

"I should ask you the same thing." The blonde was still staring at him wide-eyed, but he ignored her, focused on his bondmate, who'd hurried to the female's side.

"I... Damn it, Aiden! You ruined the surprise." She grabbed him by the hand and tugged him inside, shutting the door behind him.

He flicked a glance to the female, who looked oddly familiar. He'd seen eyes like hers...every freaking day when he looked in the mirror. "Who are you?" he demanded, much harsher than intended.

The female just blinked rapidly, seeming almost speechless as she swiped away tears.

Larissa tucked up against him, linking her arm through his. "We're going to talk about your sneaky behavior later, but Aiden, this is Catriona, your sister."

He blinked, unsure he'd heard right. "I have a sister?"

"You really didn't know about me?" The female burst into tears.

Panic hummed through him. He turned to his mate, unsure what to say or do. He'd come here for... Hell, he wasn't sure what he'd thought he'd find. Not this. He couldn't believe he had a sister he didn't know about.

"Long story short, Catriona reached out to Connor when she discovered where you were living—against your parents' knowledge—and Connor had Ryan look into her to make sure she was really your sister. Then he came to me to set up a surprise for you for Christmas. We've been emailing and Skyping, but she just got in from Edinburgh this morning."

He could only stare.

"I'm so sorry for just showing up like this. Mum and Dad never said much about you, just that..." Catriona cleared her throat, her accent bringing up long-buried memories of his homeland. "I've always wanted to meet you, and when I turned eighteen I decided I was going to, no matter what they said."

Eighteen? Christ, he felt about a hundred looking at her. "If I'd known you existed I would have reached out a lot sooner," he rasped out. When he thought Larissa had been murdered and his own pack had turned their backs on him, he'd left and never looked back. He'd never even returned to Scotland in all these years. Hadn't even been across the pond at all.

The girl launched herself at him and he barely caught her in time. She was tall, like him, and though slender she was solid like all shifters. Wrapping his arms around her, a stunned laugh slipped out. He had a sister. *Merry Christmas.*

Thank you for this, he said to Larissa, looking at her over Catriona's shoulder.

You're welcome... You better not have thought I was coming here to meet up with a male. Her eyes narrowed ever so slightly as she eyed him. *And how did you know I was here, anyway?*

I didn't think you'd cheat. And I'll tell you the rest later. Because he was feeling too embarrassed to admit the truth now. That he'd pretty much stalked his mate using her phone.

I'm going to leave you two alone for a bit. I'll be downstairs getting tea. She was out the door before he could respond, moving with the grace and agility of someone of her power and age.

Stepping back, his sister wiped away errant tears and he wasn't ashamed to admit he had to blink back a few himself. "I don't even know where to start," he said.

"I hope you'll start by telling me I can stay for Christmas."

"Definitely. You can stay as long as you want." His heart swelled with an excess of emotions as he collapsed on one of the side chairs and she did the same, sitting on the chaise across from him. He had so many damn questions, wanted to know everything about her. Staring at her, there was no denying they were related, and if his packmate Ryan had researched her then he knew for a fact she was who she said she was.

Embarrassed as he was for having followed his mate here, he was glad he'd done it now. He'd never felt as if he was missing anything once he had Larissa in his life again, but having family he might be able to have a real relationship with?

This was the best Christmas present he could have wished for.

Reaching out, he took his sister's hand in his and she gave him the biggest smile, almost as if relieved.

Merry Christmas, indeed.

CHAPTER SEVEN

Vivian held Lucas's hand as they raced down the stairs. It was Friday afternoon and since they were so close to Christmas they didn't have school today and would be off for two weeks after that.

Two whole weeks. She couldn't wait. She'd overheard Ana and Connor talking about potentially putting her and Lucas in a human school but she hoped they didn't.

She loved it on the ranch, loved being able to shift to her jaguar anytime she needed to during school. Sometimes it was just too hard to keep her human form. She needed to run free. And okay, she loved sleeping on tree branches under a warm sun.

"Where are we going?" Lucas asked, running alongside her.

He was the best friend ever. He never told her they shouldn't do something, even if they probably shouldn't. But the way she saw it, it was better to do something and get in trouble for it later than ask to do something and be told no. She'd discovered that she got in way less trouble if she did something she hadn't been told she couldn't.

Not her fault she didn't know all the rules.

"I want to see if Esperanze can take us into town." Because she had a big secret and needed to get a last-minute present.

"For what?"

She glanced around as they reached the foyer. She scented Ana but couldn't tell if her mom was in the house or not. Technically Ana was her adopted mom, but the truth was, Vivian thought of her as her mom and had started calling her that sometimes. It felt a little weird since her own mom had died, but...she really loved Ana. And she knew with a bone-deep certainty that her own mom would have wanted her to be happy.

"I can't tell you yet," she whispered. Noel wasn't here and she knew that Connor wasn't either, but she didn't know about Ana.

"Is this something that's gonna get me in trouble? Again?" Lucas lifted an eyebrow.

She flipped her dark hair over her shoulder. "Maybe." It wasn't, but she wanted to see what he'd say.

He sighed, sounding kind of like Ryan. He'd been adopted by Ryan when he was four. She liked that she had that in common with Lucas. Whenever she was with him, she knew she belonged somewhere. "Fine. Just wanted to know ahead of time."

She snorted. "You won't get in trouble. I promise. I just want to buy a present."

Ana stepped out of the living room at that moment, looking at her cell phone, clearly distracted. She blinked when she saw them. "Hey, kiddos. I

thought you were at Ryan and Teresa's," she said, looking between them.

"We were. But I had to get something." Vivian had
just grabbed money from her piggy bank. She'd been sav-
ing for a while and was really glad she had been. Now
she wouldn't have to ask Connor for money.

"Where are you guys going?"

"To see Esperanze." It was true, she just didn't want
to tell Ana why.

"There's no school today."

"I know but we need her help with something," Lucas
said, smiling so innocently.

Vivian wondered how he pulled it off because she
never could. Ana always seemed to know when she was
up to something.

"Oh, well can I help you?"

"Nah, we're okay. I've got my cell phone with me if
you need me though." He gave that sweet smile again,
looking all guileless—a word she'd just learned in school.
It was totally appropriate for Lucas's expression right
now.

Ana just nodded and kissed both of them on the fore-
head before heading to the kitchen.

"Man, I have no idea how you do that." Vivian said
once they were outside and far enough away from the
house.

"Do what?"

"No one ever questions you about anything."

He just shot her a sideways look. He didn't have to say a word. She already knew what he was thinking. She always did. Of course no one ever questioned him because he was pretty much perfect. He never broke the rules. Not really. He bent them when he was with her though.

"So what present are you getting?"

She bit her bottom lip, looked over her shoulder and then glanced around the main yard. A few of their packmates were out, but not many. Still... "It's a secret."

He seemed intrigued, looked around with her. "Come on." He grabbed her hand and they ran for the barn.

Once they were inside they ducked into a stall that had been turned into a storage shed. "What's the secret?"

Vivian didn't bother asking Lucas not to tell anyone. He was her best friend. He'd never break her trust. "I think Ana's pregnant."

His eyes widened. "For real?"

"Yep. I found a bunch of empty pregnancy test boxes in the garbage outside."

He frowned. "Why were you in the outside garbage?"

"That doesn't matter. Once I saw those I looked in all the garbage cans in the house and found a couple of those stick thingies buried in one of the little garbage cans. They were all positive."

"That's awesome."

She was glad he thought so too. "I know. But now I have to get the baby a present."

His frown deepened. "The baby won't be here for a while."

"So what? I still need to get her something."

"Her?"

She shrugged. "I kinda hope it's a girl." The thought of having a little sister was awesome. But she'd be happy with a little brother too.

"Maybe we should ask Leila to take us into town instead of Esperanze. What if, like, Esperanze tells Ana we know?"

Vivian shook her head. "I thought of that. Leila's out with her boyfriend."

"Okay, well maybe if we beg she'll keep it a secret."

"She will." Esperanze was an awesome teacher and Vivian trusted her.

"Did you get me a present?"

"Of course." She couldn't believe he'd even asked.

He reached into his jacket pocket and pulled out something wrapped in brown paper. "I was going to wait until Christmas but...I made this for you." He shoved it at her, his cheeks flushing red.

Excitement hummed through her. She loved getting presents. When she tugged on the twine, her breath caught in her throat. "You made this?" It was a small wood carving of a wolf who looked exactly like Lucas, and a much smaller jaguar who looked just like her. It was so beautiful and detailed.

He nodded and kicked at the dusty ground. A couple pieces of hay moved. He seemed almost embarrassed, though she wasn't sure why. His gift was incredible.

"This is the best thing anyone's ever given me. I love it." She threw her arms around his neck and hugged him tight. "I'm glad we're best friends."

"Me too."

"Do you want your present tonight, or do you want to wait until Christmas?" she asked, stepping back. He had way more patience than her so she guessed he'd wait.

He half-grinned as if he read her mind. "I'll wait."

"Okay. You ready to find Esperanze?"

"Yep." He grabbed her hand in his and they ran out together.

Just like always, whenever they held hands, her jaguar was completely peaceful and happy. Deep down, she knew they'd be best friends forever.

* * *

December glanced around the area behind her house. On the ranch they didn't have fenced-in yards and she wanted to make sure no one could see her when she shifted back to her human form.

Which was still a surreal thought for her to have. After giving birth six months ago she was now able to shift into a wolf.

A motherfreaking wolf.

It was nuts and incredible at the same time. So she did it as often as she could, running around in wolf form everywhere and anywhere she was able.

That didn't mean she was okay with the whole nudity thing that so many of her packmates were fine with.

She did not relish the idea of showing her breasts to someone then sitting across the table from them at a Sunday dinner. The only person who would see her naked was her mate, Liam. Once she was sure the coast was clear, she shifted back, letting the change come over her in a rush of magical warmth.

Breathing hard, she pushed up to her feet and hurried inside. She'd left her clothes folded neatly on the kitchen counter before heading out and was glad they were still there. Sometimes Liam liked to move them so she had to run around the house naked.

And if she was naked then he inevitably got naked too. Not that there was a thing wrong with that. She smiled just thinking about her delicious mate and all the ways he made her moan his name.

After tugging on her sweater and jeans, she went in search of her mate and sweet baby girl. In their living room Liam was stretched out on a recliner with six-month-old Ellie tucked right in the crook of his arm.

With broad shoulders and standing about six feet, two inches, the male looked like a linebacker. Right now he was shirtless and showing off the tattoo on his chest of his family crest. It was hard to believe that at one time she'd tried to resist this male.

He smiled a little sleepily at her. "How was the run?" he asked quietly.

"Exhilarating. It's so cold out, I love it." She grabbed a throw blanket and tucked it around him and Ellie before she kissed him. Just a lazy meeting of mouths she wished could turn in to more.

But not with a sleeping baby in the house. It was just the way things were. If they started getting frisky it was like Ellie had radar and would wake up demanding to be changed, fed or any number of things.

So December stretched out on the couch nearest him and grabbed another throw blanket, pulled it over herself. She smiled at the two people who meant more to her than anything. A year ago she never could have imagined this life for herself, that she'd be mated to a shifter, be a shifter herself and have the sweetest baby girl in the world.

"So, I think I know a secret before you do." Liam gave her a grin, all sexy smugness.

She just snorted and tucked an arm behind her head. "Somehow I doubt that." Everyone in the pack seemed to tell her their secrets. Which she didn't actually mind. She loved how welcoming everyone had been, and she never doubted that she was a full-fledged, accepted member of this pack even if she hadn't been born a shifter.

"I overheard the cubs talking in the barn. They thought they were alone and I didn't mean to eavesdrop but...Vivian thinks Ana's pregnant."

December jolted up. "For real?"

He nodded, smug grin still in place and growing wider. "Yep. Can't believe I found out before you."

"Does Connor know?" Because she was surprised his brother hadn't told him.

"I don't think so. He's been so damn busy lately, but no, he'd have told me." He shifted slightly when Ellie made little gurgling sounds in her sleep.

"Knowing Ana, she's probably going to tell him on Christmas morning as a surprise." Ana was one of the first shifters to make her feel truly welcome into the pack and December adored her.

"Sounds about right. So...you ready for another one?"

She blinked, surprised by the question. "Ah...maybe in a couple years." She loved Ellie and couldn't imagine her life without her daughter, but babies were hard work. And she and Liam had help from all of their pack-mates. She had new respect for single parents going it alone. "Why, are you ready?"

Giving her a wicked grin she knew oh so well, he quietly stood and set Ellie in her bassinet near the Christmas tree. Their little girl barely moved, telling December she was exhausted. Which could be a very good thing for them right now. Maybe they actually would sneak in a little grownup time.

"I was thinking we could at least practice today." His deep voice twined around her, made all her nerve endings flare to life. She swore the male's voice was an aphrodisiac.

"Practice?" she murmured, throwing her blanket off her body.

"Oh, yeah. Lots and lots of practice." He let out a soft growl before he climbed on top of her, stretching his huge body over hers on the couch.

She wrapped her arms and legs around him, his body now as familiar to her as her own. Arching into him as their mouths met, she let out a quiet moan of pleasure at the simple feel of him. This protective, powerful male had stolen her heart a little over a year ago and she was looking forward to many, many more years together.

CHAPTER EIGHT

Nathan stretched his legs out on the bench, inhaled the crisp winter air outside. Noel should be getting out of her counseling session soon and he had a surprise for her. One he hoped she liked.

On Friday they'd made decorations for the Christmas tree, and some of the other guys and even cubs had joined in. It meant they hadn't gotten any alone time when they watched movies later that night, but he was okay with that.

He just wanted to spend time with her, to get to know the female he'd started to fall for a year ago. His wolf had already completely accepted her and he knew what that meant. He was just waiting for Noel's wolf to catch up and realize they were mates.

So when she'd hesitantly asked him to come with her to this session, he'd jumped at the chance. He understood what a big deal it was, that she was letting him into this part of her life.

When the front door of the clinic—which was actually a house—opened, he stood as Noel stepped out, wrapping a red and white scarf around her neck. "Hey. I was wondering where you were."

"Just wanted to sit out in the fresh air. How'd everything go?"

"Good." Her body language and scent were relaxed as she linked her arm through his.

He subtly inhaled, letting her amber and vanilla scent wrap around him as they descended the short set of stairs and started down the walkway to the sidewalk.

The doctor's office was in a quiet part of downtown, nestled in between other professionals' offices which were also homes. Dusk was falling and everything was relatively quiet, most of the businesses having closed an hour ago. Snow covered most of the lawns but all the roads and sidewalks had been cleared off.

"It's nice to have someone to talk to. Someone who didn't know Carmen."

He noticed that she had no problem saying her sister's name, seemed more okay talking about her, and he was glad.

"It makes a difference." It had taken him a long time to get to that point. "I go to Aiden if I need to talk about my family. Or anything, really." It had been ages since he had, but Aiden had always been the easiest packmate to talk to.

Noel smiled softly. "Yeah, I can see that. He's a good wolf. Now you have me...if you ever need to talk about them. Or just want to. I'd love to know more about your family anyway."

He'd already opened up to her in the past few days and planned to continue to do so. "I will." He didn't want to talk about the past right now though. No, he had something else entirely in mind. "I, uh, have a surprise for you. One I think you'll like."

Excitement lit her gaze. "Yeah?" She held his arm just a little tighter and he savored the connection.

"Near the ski lodge there's a drive-in theater showing Christmas movies the next couple days."

A soft smile lifted her full, kissable lips. "My mom took us to those when we were kids. We'd all sit in the back of my dad's truck and watch them together."

"I'm surprised your Alpha was okay with that." He only knew what she'd told him about her father, how he'd been set in his ways.

She laughed lightly, leaned her head against his shoulder for a brief moment as they walked. "That was one of the few arguments my mom won. He was so weird about us not integrating with the human world. As if..." She sighed. "I really don't know what his problem was. And sometimes I feel guilty that I'm glad Connor's my Alpha now." She shot him a sideways glance, as if afraid he'd judge her for the words she didn't say.

Nathan didn't think Noel was glad her father was dead, but she clearly liked Connor as an Alpha better than her own father.

From past experience he was aware that Connor was one of the best types of Alphas out there. He treated everyone like they mattered, understood that the betas, who many Alphas saw as weak, were the true backbone of any pack. They had level heads for the most part and kept packs running smoothly on a day-to-day basis in a way that most shifters didn't have the temperament for. There was something in Alphas, true ones, that called to them to take care of others. "I'm glad to have him as an Alpha too."

"Do you remember the first drive-in theater?"

He snorted. Close to reaching one hundred, he'd been a teenager when the first had come to his town. He'd lost his pack not long after that. "I actually do." And that made him feel a thousand freaking years old. He'd seen so many changes in the last century.

A few blocks over they reached his truck. She'd wanted him to park farther away so she could walk, have more time with him before seeing the doctor. And he liked spending any extra time with her.

On the ride to the drive-in theater they talked, mainly about their favorite movies. She might not have seen the Star Wars movies—which he was going to remedy soon—but she was a movie nerd like him. One more thing for him to adore about her.

"I can't believe they're playing Die Hard." She took the quilt he handed her from the extended cab while he pulled out the small cooler and back pillows.

He tossed them into the bed of the truck. "It's the best Christmas movie." He'd seen his share over the decades and Die Hard would always be a favorite. And people who thought it wasn't a holiday movie were wrong.

"I *know*. I'm just glad they're not playing some awful black and white movie. You know, from your era." She whispered the last part, snickering as she tucked the quilt under her arm.

"Age references, really?" He grabbed another blanket and shut the door.

Laughing, she walked to the back of the truck. "I've got to have my fun."

He was glad she was having fun, loved her teasing—had missed this facet of her personality the last year. He'd parked with the bed facing the big screen so they'd be able to stretch out. "Any more age references and I might not share what's in the cooler."

Her eyes lit up at that. "Food?"

"Yep. And drinks. I brought your favorite cider."

She blinked in surprise. "I can't believe you remember that."

Oh, he remembered every single conversation they'd ever had, had replayed them all in his mind too many times to count. He lifted a shoulder before taking the edge of the quilt she was holding.

Together they stretched it out and climbed up into the bed of the truck. He pulled the tailgate up as she set up the back pillows.

"This was a good idea," she said, motioning to the pillows.

He just grinned and opened the cooler. They were a little early but other vehicles were starting to arrive, pulling in around them, thankfully with enough space in between that they weren't on top of each other.

Noel stretched out her legs, watching him with undeniable appreciation as he pulled out two thermoses.

"What's in there?"

"Apple cider in this one, hot soup in this one and..." He pulled out a small container and popped the lid off. "Cream cheese penguins."

Noel grinned at the sight of the little penguins made from black olives, cream cheese and little red pepper strips for their scarves. "Did you make these? They're adorable."

He cleared his throat. "It was December's idea. And...she made them for me." He hadn't been able to make the olive heads stay on right.

"Thank you," she said as he handed her a mug of cider. "For more than just the drink. For tonight, for everything."

He wasn't sure what she meant by everything, but he nodded. This was part of courting his future mate. Whether she realized that was what she was to him or not. He didn't plan to stop courting her even after they were mated either.

Because Noel was his female, and he wanted to keep making her happy for the rest of their lives.

* * *

Angelo growled low in his throat as Brianna shifted on her feet nervously. His mate had been acting nervous all day and it was making his wolf edgy. "They'll be here soon. Everything will be fine."

A female voice came over the loudspeaker at the small airport, telling everyone one of the incoming flights had been delayed by fifteen minutes. The flight they were waiting on.

Petite and adorable, his fae mate looked up at him with something he'd never seen in her gaze before. Something he couldn't define. And the riot of scents that rolled off her were too many for him to sift through. "I recently turned down a job she asked us to go on." Her soft lilting Irish accent wrapped around him.

It took a lot to surprise him, but the indefinable scents on her and this news did just that. "When did you turn it down?"

"A week ago."

He frowned. "You didn't tell me?"

"I was going to." She bit her bottom lip, looked away from him and toward the wide glass doors where all passengers eventually exited.

But? He asked along their telepathic link, waiting for her to continue.

Instead of responding she just kept chewing on her bottom lip, staring at the doors. Brianna was never nervous about anything but he was pretty sure that was what was going on now.

Which didn't make sense. She'd seen her family since mating with him. They hadn't been thrilled at first, but they'd finally adjusted to it. Her family was part of the Tuatha, the royal line of the fae, ancient and brutal. Oh yeah, he'd gotten himself hitched to a princess.

A very strong, smart one. She didn't have the extrasensory abilities he did, but she could harness lightning-like energy and destroy anyone she wanted with it. She could also heal others under certain circumstances. She'd long since proved her trustworthiness to the pack even before they'd mated, had the loyalty of even Jayce since she'd killed the male who'd tortured and nearly killed his beloved Kat. Hell, she could even subtly influence humans to bend to her will. She was incredible.

His female did not do scared or nervous.

Until today.

"Sweetheart?" he asked, wrapping an arm around her shoulders. "You're going to have to tell me what's going on in your head right now."

She was stiff, staring straight ahead and still not looking at him. "I need to tell you something. But now is not the time." In the ten months since they'd been mated, some of her formal speech patterns had relaxed, but she occasionally fell back into that formality he found sexy as hell.

The first time they'd met he thought she was haughty, had gotten off on making him crazy. Then he'd realized none of that was true—that the petite blonde had just been nervous around him.

"Now isn't the time, huh?" He leaned down, subtly inhaled her sweetness. *Would it be appropriate to grab a quickie in the nearest bathroom?* he asked along their link. He knew the question was certain to rile her up.

She snapped her head up to stare at him, her bright blue eyes wide. "I'm pregnant," she blurted, fear lacing those two words.

He blinked once. Twice. Then a grin split his face. "We're having a cub?" Joy like he'd never known punched through him. They hadn't been trying. Well, they hadn't been *not* trying either, considering how often they made love. But a mating between their species was so damn rare.

"The baby could be fae. I just do not know how a shifter-fae child will...turn out." Her voice trembled.

"I don't care if the baby's fae or shifter or a mix of both of us. I just care that he or she is healthy." Could she really doubt that?

"I know that." Her voice broke on the last word, her eyes welling with tears.

Needing to touch her, to comfort her, he pulled her into his arms. Screw whoever might be watching them. He tuned out everyone at the airport, gripping her tight as he buried his face against her neck.

"My hormones are going crazy," she whispered against his chest. "I've never felt like this, so out of control and scared. Having a baby... I just didn't expect it to happen so fast or maybe even at all." The fae didn't conceive as easily as shifters. "And I never expected to be afraid."

"You can be as crazy as you want. And we're in this together. You've got me and a whole pack to support you, and if that means we stop taking jobs for your family for a while, that's fine. And hell, I'm afraid too," he murmured against the top of her head. "I think that's what happens when you become a parent." Or an almost-parent. Because holy shit, a kid? Yeah, that was a little scary to think about.

Sniffling, she pulled back and gave him a watery smile. He cupped her cheeks, swiped away the falling tears. It was so strange to see his mate crying, and his wolf was going crazy, clawing and snarling and demanding that Angelo make it stop, to fix this.

"I found out a week ago and I wanted to tell you. I just didn't know how."

He brushed his lips over hers, not caring that she'd waited a week. It was a huge deal, and if she'd needed to come to terms with it, he understood. "This is pretty much the best Christmas present you could have ever gotten me."

"I guess I'll return your present, then." She said it so deadpan, it took him a moment to realize she was joking.

A bark of laughter escaped him. His mate didn't make jokes often. It wasn't part of her nature. He pulled her into his arms again, half-listened as an announcement was made that various flights would be disembarking soon.

"That was their flight number," she said, a hint of nerves flickering in her gaze again.

"You want to tell them?" Her mother and brothers were coming to visit for a couple weeks. Thankfully, not staying at their house. They'd rented a place instead.

He liked them all well enough, but he didn't want to have to hold back with his mate for a couple weeks. Keeping his hands off her was impossible.

She sucked in a steadying breath, nodded. "At dinner tonight."

"We'll tell them together, then." Taking her hand in his, he turned toward the glass doors as they opened and people starting streaming out.

He couldn't believe they were going to be parents soon, that he was going to have a child with the female he loved more than anything.

Falling for a fae had never been in his plans, but he'd known from pretty much the start that she was the female for him. And when he'd thought she'd planned to go back to Ireland without him, he'd intended to follow her. Because he'd follow her anywhere, even to the afterlife.

Now they were about to start their own family. *I love you.* He streamed the words along their telepathic link, more raw emotion than actual words.

"I love you too," she whispered, gripping his hand tightly.

CHAPTER NINE

Parker wiped a sweaty palm on his jeans, inwardly cursed himself. He was a grown man and the sheriff of this town.

None of that seemed to matter around Maria Cordona. Whenever he was near her, he felt like a sweaty, nervous teenager.

Taking a deep breath, he opened the door to the bookstore his sister, December, owned. Maria was working tonight, so like usual for the last six months, he was bringing her a drink. Tonight it was hot cocoa. Sometimes it was iced green tea or coffee or whatever he thought she might be in the mood for.

Standing at one of the display shelves, she glanced over her shoulder and grinned when she saw him. "Hey, Sheriff."

Laughing, he strode toward her and held out the tray. One hot cocoa for her and a coffee for him. "I'm not on duty tonight."

"I can see that, Parker." Her eyes flicked over his sweater, leather jacket and jeans before meeting his gaze again, that dark gaze sultry and teasing.

All the muscles in his body pulled taut, as was usual around her, especially when she said his name. Shifters had exceptional scenting abilities and he had no idea if she could smell his lust. At this point, he didn't care. He wanted her to know how much she affected him. They'd become friends about six months ago, not too long after she'd lost her sister.

At one time he'd hated shifters because of the way his brother had been murdered. But Maria's sister had been murdered by a human and she didn't hate all humans.

Because that would be freaking stupid, she'd told him once when he'd questioned her about it.

He still felt shame for the way he'd reacted to his sister's relationship with Liam at first. Thankfully things were good between them now.

At the moment he was hoping for a Christmas miracle, that the funny, slightly sarcastic Maria would want to go on a date with him. He'd been trying to ask for six damn months but for some reason just couldn't man up and do it. Deep down it was because he wanted more than a date.

He wanted everything from this woman. She'd blindsided him with her funny attitude and quick wit, and after two weeks of being friends, he'd known he wanted a 'til death do us part kind of relationship. He'd just never expected to fall for a shifter. But blaming an entire species for the actions of one was stupid. Unfortunately he'd been stupid for too damn long. Not anymore, however.

"How's work tonight?"

A slight shrug. "Good. A lot of customers are disappointed that the Erin action figures are gone, but December ordered a new box that should be in a couple days after Christmas at least."

He snorted. "I heard what Kat did. How's Erin taking it?"

"Pretty sure she's plotting her revenge."

"Would you like to go to dinner with me when you get off work?" Tomorrow was Christmas Eve so the store was closing up at six tonight. And yeah, it was last minute and he knew he should have given her more notice.

"Yes." She didn't even pause in her answer.

He blinked. He needed to make sure she understood he wanted more than friendship. "As in a date."

"I know. Been waiting for you to ask me out for six long months, *Sheriff*," she murmured, putting emphasis on his title as she stepped closer. She set her cup down on the nearby display shelf. "You know how many times I've touched myself thinking about you?" The question was a sharp, bold and unexpected demand.

One that had his entire body reacting. She'd fantasized about him? His cock jerked against his pants and he nearly dropped his drink. That was the hottest thing she could have said to him. He blindly set the coffee down on the same shelf before sliding his hands around her waist, pulled her close. He didn't bother fighting the groan at the feel of her in his arms. God, holding her like this was like holding a piece of heaven. She was all soft curves and lush feminine scent. "Hopefully as many times as me."

"What took you so long to ask me out?" she murmured, arching slightly into him, her breathing erratic and her pupils dilated. "My wolf likes to be chased, but I've been getting very, very impatient. I thought I might have to take drastic measures to get you to notice me."

She might be a beta female, but he'd learned that didn't mean what he thought it had. Betas ran the gamut in their personalities. They were just slightly weaker than alphas in actual strength. She might not be as physically strong as others in her pack, but she was all sass and sexiness. "I want more than a date, Maria. I'm not in this for something casual." His grip around her tightened, possessiveness swelling inside him like it always did around her. He'd learned that shifters liked people to be blunt. Even if they didn't, he couldn't hold back.

Not with her. Not about this.

"Good, because neither am I."

He crushed his mouth to hers, taking and tasting what he'd been dreaming about for months. By this time next year he planned to have a ring on her finger and claim her for everyone to see. Human and supernatural alike.

Because she was his. And he'd chase her for the rest of their damn lives if her wolf wanted it. He'd do whatever she wanted. She was a female worth fighting for.

* * *

"Dude, Parker and Maria? I wondered when that would happen." Kat linked her arm through Jayce's as they headed down Main Street. They'd just had the best dinner and she felt like going home and falling into a food coma. But they had other stuff to take care of tonight.

"I'm surprised it took him so long." Her sexy mate half-smiled, the action out of character for him except when he was with her or their adopted daughter, Leila.

It wasn't like Leila called them Mom and Dad; that would be a little strange, given that she'd been sixteen when they'd taken her in, and she had been deeply loved by her parents. But they'd made things official so that no matter what, Leila would always have a family, always have a place to belong. In the shifter world that was important. Her own parents had been murdered because they'd been packless and unprotected and had refused to pay protection money to thugs.

"So, I heard you reached out to Leila's boyfriend yesterday."

Jayce's expression darkened, but he nodded. "Yeah. Invited the fucker to Christmas dinner."

"And do you plan on introducing him as 'the fucker' to everyone?" She kept a straight face as she asked.

Which earned her a scowl from him as they continued down the sidewalk. She was aware of holiday shoppers creating a subtle path for them on the sidewalk, but figured Jayce didn't even notice it at this point.

With a shaved head, a wicked-looking scar on his face, and intense gunmetal gray eyes that had seen far more death than any individual should, the male screamed danger. And to Kat, he screamed raw sex appeal. She'd never forget the first time they'd met—and the first time she'd put him in his place.

"I just don't get why she's with a human. He's weaker than her."

Kat snorted. "She's a teenager. And he rides a motorcycle and has tattoos." It wasn't that hard to see. At least not to Kat.

"I want her with someone strong. He doesn't even have to be a shifter. Just someone stronger." The frowning continued.

His logic was something she actually understood. She wouldn't have a year ago, but now that she'd been entrenched in the shifter world, having been turned herself, she appreciated what he wanted for Leila. He wanted someone who could literally have Leila's back, who'd be able to be her equal in all matters, especially the physical ones. They lived in a violent world sometimes and Jayce just wanted her to have a mate who could back her up. She could respect that.

"Baby, this isn't the male she'll be with long-term. Trust me," she murmured, stepping around an elderly couple on the sidewalk so they wouldn't have to move.

"How can you know?" He scrubbed his free hand over the back of his neck.

She snorted again. "I just do. She started dating him mainly, I think, to rile you up. You push her so hard in training and..." Kat figured this human boy was a way to let Leila rebel slightly. She was an enforcer-in-training and a gifted hacker and almost, but not quite eighteen. Even when she turned eighteen she'd still be considered a cub for a while, at least by pack standards. She needed an outlet. Kat wasn't sure how to word that to make Jayce understand, though, so she said, "Now that you've outwardly accepted him I have a feeling their relationship will be short-lived."

Surprise clear on his face, he turned to her. "That doesn't even make sense."

"Teenagers don't make sense."

He just grumbled to himself as they continued down brightly lit Main Street. She loved it down here around the holidays. Last year she'd worked at one of the local ski lodges and had spent most of her time on the mountain. She loved being able to be part of the town more now.

"All right, try not to snarl too much if her boyfriend is with her," Kat murmured as he opened a glass door to the local hardware store.

It was almost closing time and they were picking up a box of books the owner was donating. Kat, and now Leila too, volunteered at the local literacy center. About once a month various local business donated boxes of books, usually new. She and Jayce had picked up most of the boxes yesterday but were down here to grab a straggler tonight.

"What took you slackers so long?" Leila asked, leaning against the glass countertop, clearly having been talking to the owner's teenage daughter, who smiled at Kat—and gave Jayce a wary look.

"Dinner at Kelly's." Jayce shot her a grin. "And we stopped at Clara's Ice Cream shop afterward."

"Without me?" She pushed up from the countertop, her gray eyes filled with annoyance, and a trace of hurt.

"He's messing with you," Kat murmured. Jayce and Leila went to the ice cream place at least once a week. Usually three times, and ate far too much. It was like their little ritual, one Kat knew that Leila held dear. More than a trainer, he was her mentor and father figure as well.

"Where's your boyfriend?" Jayce's voice was butter smooth, no hint of the annoyance she knew was lingering beneath the surface. "I thought he was going to come with you tonight."

"Oh, ah, we broke up." She lifted a shoulder.

Told you! Kat shouted along their telepathic link, unable to hide her smugness.

Now Jayce full-on growled. "Did he hurt you?"

Leila laughed and rolled her eyes with the flair only a teenager could manage. "Please. Now, if you two are ready, let's get this show on the road. I'm hungry." She turned to the girl at the counter. "Thank your dad again for these books. I'll see you at the New Year's thing?"

The human teenager, who had Korean roots like Leila, nodded, her grin widening. "Definitely."

Jayce lifted the box, carrying it in front of him as if it were empty, and they headed out again. He cleared his throat as they stepped onto the sidewalk. "So, what's happening on New Year's?"

Another casual shrug. "Party thing with some human friends."

Kat wrapped her arm around Leila's shoulders. "I'm glad you're making friends." Later she'd find out where the party was and who would be there, but the truth was, Leila could take care of herself better than some full-grown shifters, and Kat and Jayce had to show her they trusted her. "Want to talk about your breakup?"

"Not really... Can we stop by December's Book Nook before getting ice cream? I want to pick something up."

"No problem." Jayce moved in front of them on the sidewalk to make room for a cluster of laughing teenagers headed in the opposite direction. "Then you can tell us about your breakup. I need to make sure this boy didn't hurt you." His words were low, but they had no problem hearing him with their shifter senses. There was no room for argument in his voice either.

Leila rolled her eyes to Kat, but she also half-smiled. Jayce might not completely understand how to talk to teenagers, especially teenage girls, but he understood Leila, understood their family dynamic. And for him, for all of them, they didn't often have secrets. Kat also knew that while Leila would never say it out loud, she was glad that Jayce cared enough to be protective of her.

Something Kat was grateful for as well. She loved her newly adopted pack, but Leila and Jayce were her immediate family now. They were still learning as they went with a lot of things, but more than anything, they always communicated with each other. Sometimes, according to Leila, it was too much.

But Kat knew the girl liked how open they all were with each other.

I have a feeling she broke up with him, Kat said along their telepathic link. *She's not nearly sad enough about it.*

Good. I won't have to see his stupid face over Christmas dinner now.

Kat nearly snorted aloud at her mate's words, but contained herself. "So, you guys want to guess how many pregnancies we have at the ranch right now?"

Leila's eyes widened and Jayce just cocked an eyebrow as he fell back in step with them.

"What? It's not like I can help knowing." She'd been a seer as a human, literally seeing things not visible to the human eye, but under the surface of a person. It was how she'd known about shifters, vampires and other things that went bump in the night long before they'd come out to the world. The same gift translated to other things, including seeing the spark of new life in pregnant women. It was like a little glow and only happened after a certain stage in the pregnancy. She wasn't even sure of the science to it, because she hadn't known when December had been pregnant in the beginning stages.

"Four?" Jayce asked.

"Three," Leila said.

Kat shook her head, grinned. "Five." And one of those pregnancies was going to be a huge deal. All cubs were a big deal, but the Alpha and his mate having a baby? Pretty huge news.

"Who?" Leila asked.

Kat just grinned as they reached the bookstore. "My lips are sealed." And maybe in a few years she and Jayce would have one or two or half a dozen. But for now, she was enjoying her family and wickedly sexy mate.

Pretty sure I have ways of making you talk. Jayce's voice was dark and sensual along their telepathic link, that rich chocolate scent of his lust making her lightheaded for a moment.

Give it your best shot. No matter what he did, she'd be a winner. Because having Jayce worship her naked body? Oh yeah. She'd take his brand of torture every day of the week.

CHAPTER TEN

Nathan stepped out of the shared bathroom, a towel wrapped around his waist, and paused as Noel's scent permeated the hallway.

Frowning, he stepped out into the living room, surprised to see her sitting on the couch, a hot cup of cocoa in her hand as she talked to his packmate, Jacob. His very single packmate. The Christmas tree they'd decorated was lit and the fire crackled, giving a soft, romantic glow to the room. Yeah, Jacob needed to be gone like ten minutes ago.

Noel turned at either the sound of his footsteps—which he doubted because he was ghost-silent—or because she'd scented him too. Her amber eyes darkened as she raked an appreciative gaze over his bare chest.

Pleasure swelled in his chest as she blatantly checked him out, the hunger there so vivid it made him forget how to speak. For only a second.

"What the hell are you doing here?" he snarled at Jacob, knowing that 1) he sounded like a crazy jackass since Jacob *lived* here; and 2) he didn't much give a fuck. The mating heat was starting to ride him hard now that the walls between Noel and he had come down. He didn't want his single packmate looking at her, much less talking to her while they sat on a couch a foot away from each other. And he didn't care if he was acting like a caveman throwback to his ancestors.

Noel let out a small gasp as Jacob's mouth dropped open. Just as quickly the obnoxious male grinned and shoved up from the couch. Sighing, he shook his head. "Another one bites the dust." A grin on his face, he nodded at Noel, murmured a polite goodbye before turning to Nathan. "You'll have the place to yourself tonight."

With that, the other male shut the front door behind him. Nathan was aware of Noel standing and setting her mug down while he quickly locked the front door. No one would be interrupting them. She hadn't come out and said it but he was almost positive that this was the night things changed between them, the night he sank into her sweet body, the night he claimed her.

"I know we didn't have plans until later, but I thought it would be okay if I stopped by early. I missed you today." Noel's hesitant voice made him realize she didn't understand what was going on with him.

Probably because he'd never acted this possessive before. "You can come by anytime you want. You could move in with me tomorrow if you wanted." He inwardly winced at his not-so-smooth words. *Way to be subtle about things.*

Her mouth parted slightly and he took that as all the invitation he needed. Screw subtlety. This female was his and it was time he showed her that. Erasing the distance from the door to the couch in seconds, he closed his hands around her hips, tugging her flush against him.

She molded to him without pause, her hands sliding up his chest and around his neck. The feel of her fingers skating over his skin was pure heaven. They'd made plans to have dinner together tonight but now he had something else entirely in mind if she was ready.

"Too many clothes," he growled against her mouth.

Laughing lightly, she pulled back. "I've never seen you like this." Her breathing was erratic, her eyes shades darker than normal as she looked up at him, her wolf peeking through.

The hunger punching through him was a byproduct of the mating heat but... "This is who I am. I'm not normally jealous but I'll always be possessive and protective of you. That won't change." Wolves were more primal than humans by nature, but he still wanted her to know the truth of who he was. To go into this relationship with her eyes wide open.

"Good." The word was a breathy whisper. Eyes going heavy-lidded, she lifted the hem of her cream-colored sweater and tugged it over her head.

He forgot to breathe as he drank in the sight of her. The scrap of material covering her breasts shouldn't even be called a bra. Little black lace triangles barely covered her hard, pink nipples. His cock was rock hard, the towel around his waist doing nothing to hide his reaction to her.

Not that he wanted to.

She was his. And while they might not be bonding tonight, he was damn sure going to claim the female—if she'd have him.

"I want to mark you tonight," he growled out. More than want, he *needed* to rake his teeth against her skin, to give her his mark. It would be temporary. Only bonding was permanent. But temporary was better than nothing right now and it would show their pack that she was his. He didn't even trust himself to touch her again until he got the okay from her.

In response, she unbuttoned her jeans and started to push them down, but that was the go-ahead he needed from her. Well, that and the heady scent of hunger rolling off her, making his wolf wild and just a bit out of control.

He took over. Moving swiftly, he had her on her back, stretched out in front of the Christmas tree, the lights flickering off her almost bare body.

She stretched out, making the sweetest sound as he tugged her jeans and panties fully off. Oh yeah, this was what he'd been fantasizing about for a year.

His female splayed out like an offering to him and only him. There would be no other for him, that much he was certain of. Had been since pretty much the moment he'd met her.

"If I'm going to be naked, so are you." Sitting up, she grasped his towel, yanked it free so that it fell to the ground.

When her eyes widened at the sight of his erection, he felt a hundred feet tall at the pleasure that played across her features. Letting one of his claws free, he carefully sliced through the front of her bra. He'd buy her a new one. A hundred more if she wanted. But he couldn't go another second without seeing her fully naked.

Before the material had fallen away from her, she grasped his cock, taking him by surprise.

Groaning, he rolled his hips into her hold, breathing hard as she stroked him. For several moments he stared down at her working him, watching her hand wrapped around his length. All the muscles in his body were pulled tight, the pleasure of her soft touch almost too much.

"Noel," he rasped out, gripping her hand and stilling it.

She looked at him, all sultry heat and hunger even though he knew she was a virgin. Which was why he was going to make damn sure she came before he ever got inside her. He wasn't screwing things up with her.

Shifters were damn superstitious and even if they weren't bonding tonight, this was still their first time together. He would make it perfect for her. He refused to give her anything less.

"Gotta taste you." The words tore from his throat, a savage growl. It was the only warning he gave her before he had her back on the soft blankets by the tree, his face between her legs.

She let out a gasp of surprise, but slid her fingers through his hair as he inhaled her exotic scent. It was wild and spicier than normal tonight. Though he wanted to, he didn't just bury his face into her pussy. He needed to make sure she was ready, to work her up more.

Gently, he flicked his tongue up her slick folds, barely touching her.

She squirmed, her fingers tightening against his scalp even more, with just the hint of claw. The prick of pain only added to how turned on he was.

Keeping his wolf at bay, keeping himself under control until she was primed, was necessary. He flicked his tongue against her again, his teasing soft and gentler than he'd ever been with anyone else. She was sweet, her taste unique, making him think of the desert under a moonlit sky.

"Nathan, more." Her needy voice cut through his thoughts, the hunger he heard there raw and real.

She might be a virgin but she was a shifter like him, had the same primal needs. Moving slowly, he slid a finger inside her, groaning as her inner walls clenched around him.

Her moan mixed with his. And as he dragged his finger back out, he flicked his tongue right over her clit, shuddering when she did. Her entire body trembled and she tried to clench her thighs around his head, to ease the ache he knew was between her legs. She could suffocate him and he'd die a happy male.

Adding another finger, he increased his pace, stroking faster in and out of her.

"Just like that." Her words were choppy, her breathing even more wild and erratic. Her inner walls clenched convulsively around him and he knew it wouldn't take long to push her over the edge.

There was still so much more he wanted to do to her, to kiss and lick her everywhere, to learn every single inch of her body. He knew there would be time for that later, had to remind himself of patience.

Her climax was the most important thing now. Her first one by him. And not the last, as far as he was concerned.

He planned to go to sleep with her every night and wake up with her every morning—because he wasn't letting her go. The past week he'd fallen far harder for her than he had a year ago.

She'd let down the walls between them, gone out of her way to do sweet, unexpected things for him. Things he'd never imagined. Making Christmas ornaments with her had given him a peek of what life would be like with her, and yeah, he simply wasn't letting her go. She was fun and giving and had such a big heart. And if she fell back into depression, he'd be there for her. Always.

As the humans said, he was in this for better or for worse.

"Oh, Nathan!" Her breathing rasped in and out, the slick inner walls of her tight sheath rippling around his fingers.

Suddenly she arched her back and he felt the moment when she lost control, her climax pushing her over the edge. He sucked on her clit, adding even more pressure with his tongue.

Crying out his name, she rolled her hips against his face, her movements so unabashed and sensual his wolf was shoving at the surface, repeating one word in his head, again and again.

Mate.

Something he knew without a doubt.

As she grew lax under him, he lifted his head, moved up her body like a predator, wanting to claim her right then. He cupped one breast, lazily teased a nipple, savoring the way she continued to tremble and shudder under him.

She wrapped her arms and legs around him, was pulling his mouth down to hers even as he mirrored her movements. His lips crushed against hers and he was glad she could taste herself on him.

Reaching between their bodies, she grasped his hard cock. "Mine," she growled out, her wolf in her voice.

He couldn't respond, couldn't even think about forming words.

"In me, now." A soft, sensual demand from the female who completely owned him.

Slightly shifting his hips, he nudged her soft, slick entrance, hating that it might hurt. Shifters were built different than humans but it was still her first time, and the last thing he ever wanted to do was hurt this female.

Even a second's hurt was too much.

Arching up, she wrapped her legs fully around him and dug her feet into his ass as she impaled herself on him.

"Fuck!" He groaned at the feel of her tight sheath wrapped snug around his cock.

"You were taking too long," she whispered, her gaze dark on his.

There was no hint of pain there either. Still, he was going to do this right. Keeping his gaze pinned to hers, wanting to watch her as he came, wanting her to see how much she meant to him, how much she affected him, he pulled his hips back.

Her mouth parted slightly, her eyes heavy-lidded as he pushed back into her. The whimper of pleasure that escaped her soothed all of him, even as his entire body was pulled taut in anticipation.

"Want to mark you." He was asking even as his wolf snarled and clawed at his insides, demanding he take. But he would never take what wasn't freely given. It would destroy this beautiful bond forming between them. And that, he would never do. He'd rather cut off a limb.

"You'd better." Another demanding growl, her amber eyes sparking like wild starbursts.

He crushed his mouth to hers once again, unable to hold back now. She'd given him the green light and he was taking it, taking all of her.

He could feel her building to another orgasm, her inner walls rippling around his cock this time instead of his fingers. The intense grip of her was like nothing he'd ever felt. It was as if they'd been created for each other.

His balls were pulled up tight as he held back from coming. He couldn't, not yet. Even if he was ready to release inside her. That most primal, primitive part of him reveled in the thought of marking her, of completely claiming her. His scent would be on her, in her, and everyone would *know* that she was his.

When she dug her fingers into his back, claws pricking at him, he knew she was close. It wouldn't take long to push her over the edge.

Reaching between their bodies, he rubbed her clit in a tight little pattern and she shouted his name as she continued meeting his hips, stroke for stroke.

Somehow he tore his mouth from hers and buried his face in her neck. His canines descended on instinct as he scraped against her skin, marking her again.

Mate, mate, mate.

Even though there was no full moon and they weren't bonding, they would soon. He felt it bone deep.

As he pierced the skin between her neck and shoulder, he let go of his control, his own orgasm punching through him in wave after wave of pleasure. It seemed to go on forever and he never wanted to let her go.

Eventually his surroundings returned to him, the crackling fire seeming overloud in the now quiet room.

Gently, Noel stroked her fingers up and down his back. "That was amazing." A touch of awe tinged her words.

He nuzzled her neck, made sure the wounds from his canines were fully closed before nibbling kisses along her jaw. "It's just the beginning, baby."

"Mmm, I like the sound of that." Her voice was becoming drowsy, her fingers slowing slightly as he met her mouth once again.

He needed to get a washcloth to clean between her legs, to take care of her, but for just another minute, he needed to kiss her more.

He'd been fantasizing about her for the better part of the last year. To finally have her was better than anything he'd ever imagined.

Because the reality of Noel was a sweet, giving, beautiful female who he wanted to love and protect for always. And she was his.

"I love you, Nathan," she said quietly into the darkened room when he pulled back from her. Her amber eyes were bright, her gaze steady as she looked up at him. There was no doubt there.

The simple statement was a balm to the rough edge the mating heat had caused inside him. Even more than her letting him mark her, claim her. "I love you too," he whispered, stroking her soft cheek.

Talk about the best Christmas present ever. This time next year he planned to be bonded to her, and hopefully they'd have a cub of their own on the way.

CHAPTER ELEVEN

Connor tugged Ana closer to him, loved the feel of her bare back against his chest. It was always skin to skin with them, no matter what. This female had stolen his heart over half a century ago. He'd never thought he'd get another chance with her.

With her he felt complete for the first time in his entire life. Not a mongrel with nothing to give this female. "Morning, love," he murmured before nibbling her earlobe.

She shifted against the sheets, rubbing her ass right against his growing erection. "Mmm."

Her response had him sliding his hand over her abdomen and moving lower, lower until he cupped her bare mound.

"Connor." Her voice was raspy, sleepy. "What are you doing?"

"If I need to explain, I'm not doing a very good job, am I?" He bit her earlobe again.

This time she stretched out, arching into him. He loved the feel of her body curved against his, wished they had more time like this together. It seemed they were always getting interrupted by the pack for one thing or another. Hell, who was he kidding? No matter how many times he had her it was never enough.

He groaned as she intentionally wiggled her ass against him this time, and skimmed his hand back up her stomach and over her ribs until he reached a full breast. He squeezed lightly, teased a thumb over her hard nipple and—

Bang. Bang. Bang. "It's Christmas! Wake up, wake up, wake up!"

He suppressed an irritated growl. "Maybe if we ignore her she'll go away," he murmured, teasing Ana's nipple again.

"I can hear you!" Vivian's insulted voice trailed through the door.

Ana snickered and buried her face in the pillow. She let out a frustrated groan before flipping onto her back. "We'll be down in a bit," she called out.

"No. I want to open presents now. Santa came and it's wrong to make a kid wait to open their presents. In fact, I think it counts as some sort of kid injustice."

Injustice? Ana said along their telepathic link. *Where does she get this stuff?*

Connor just snorted. "All right, we'll be down in five minutes."

"Okay. I've started the coffeemaker."

Connor ran a hand over his face. Of course she had. Because when Vivian wanted something, she got it. "Thanks, kiddo."

"I'm going to go get Noel up too!" Her pounding footsteps trailed away from the door.

"Pretty sure Noel stayed the night at Nathan's." Ana sat up and ran a hand through her thick, dark hair. Mussed all around her face, her eyes still sleepy, it took all of Connor's self-control not to kiss her senseless and finish what they'd started.

He pulled a pair of jeans from their dresser. "I heard her get in around four this morning."

"Dang, I must have been passed out," she murmured before heading to their walk-in closet.

"You were." She'd been sleeping more deeply lately, he'd noticed. And a little more often than normal. The thought made him frown, but now wasn't the time to bring it up. Shifters didn't get sick like humans did, but still...he'd been wondering about it.

Ana emerged from their closet wearing dark jeans and a red sweater that molded to her soft curves, a hint of excitement and nervousness rolling off her. The scents surprised him as she ducked into their bathroom.

He trailed after her, found her washing her face.

"You nervous about what Santa brought you?" He crossed his arms over his chest, watched her carefully. He'd had a necklace custom-made for her, couldn't wait to see it on her—it and nothing else.

Laughing lightly, she put toothpaste on her toothbrush. "I already have everything I need."

Still...she was nervous. Even if he hadn't been able to scent it, she was almost jumpy as she brushed her teeth. Then her hand trembled slightly as she rinsed off her toothbrush. "Why are you staring at me?" she asked, flicking a glance at him as she pulled out a tube of lip gloss and smoothed it on her lips.

"I can't look at my female?" He was hard just watching her, knew he needed to get under control when he heard pounding footsteps coming up the stairs again.

Ignoring his question, she lifted up on tiptoe as she passed by him and brushed her lips over his. "Be quick. We've got presents to unwrap."

Oh yeah, she was nervous about something. And he planned to find out what it was.

Ten minutes later, Ana, Vivian, Noel and Connor were downstairs. Noel was stretched out on the loveseat, a cup of coffee in her hand, looking too exhausted to even be there. She hadn't bothered to get out of her pajamas and just grunted at them when she'd stumbled into the room.

Vivian was jumping up and down by the tree as Ana started sifting through the presents. "All right, Connor gets to go first." She pulled out a shiny red box with a silver bow on it.

Vivian could hardly stand still. "But—"

"No, he goes first." There was a faint edge of steel in Ana's voice as she shook her head at Vivian.

Okay, something was definitely up. Because cubs always went first. The holiday was more for them than the adults.

Instead of questioning Ana, however, he took the gift she handed him and shredded through the paper with a claw before retracting it.

His mate's anticipation hung heavy in the air, increasing his curiosity. As the shreds of wrapping fell away, he snapped open a green gift box—and sucked in a breath.

A small baby stocking lay on top of gold-colored tissue with a note attached to the top interior of the box. His eyes widened as he read the message.

BABY ARMSTRONG WILL BE JOINING US MAY 15TH.

"You're pregnant?" he blurted, snapping his gaze to hers.

Ana nodded, tears filling her eyes.

Oh, fuck. "Are those good tears?"

As she nodded harder, the tears spilled down her cheeks. "I just found out but we're already two months along."

Using his shifter speed, he had her in his arms in seconds, holding her tight against him as the Christmas tree sparkled next to them. Seconds later Vivian's little arms were around them and then Noel's as the females all squealed in happiness.

Holy shit, we're going to have a cub, he said along their telepathic link, his chest constricting as he tried to digest the news. And they only had five months to prepare for the baby. Shifter pregnancies were shorter than humans by about two months. That didn't seem nearly enough time to get ready.

I know, I can hardly believe it. Ana's excitement flowed through their link, as pure and bright as the new snow outside on the ground. *How do you feel?*

Stunned, so happy. And...terrified. He'd practically raised his brother and had been raising Vivian, but still... A new cub.

Me too. But mainly I'm happy. I hope it's okay that I waited to tell you. I wanted it to be a big surprise.

It's more than okay.

"Now you get to open my present!" Vivian's voice seemed to be about ten octaves higher than normal this morning, her excitement over Christmas infectious. She was jumping up and down again as she grabbed a red and gold striped gift bag from under the tree. "It's for the baby so it doesn't matter which of you opens it."

Everyone froze, staring at her.

"Wait, you knew I was pregnant?" Ana asked, putting the bag in her lap as Connor moved closer to her.

Vivian nodded, her grin wide and mischievous as Noel laughed, muttering something about not being surprised.

"How?" Ana asked.

"Because I'm awesome."

Ana laughed and looked at Connor, holding up the bag. "You want to open it?"

"You do the honors." He couldn't even be surprised the little she-cat had known before he had.

Pulling out the white tissue paper Ana laughed again as she lifted out a plush stuffed jaguar with the words "World's Best Big Sister" embroidered in pink on it.

"The baby's gotta know who I am." The hint of nervousness in Vivian's voice wasn't exactly surprising. They'd adopted her but things would be changing for all of them.

He pulled her into a big hug, so damn grateful he had such a sweet daughter already. "This is the best gift," he rasped out, his voice thick with unexpected emotion.

She hugged him back as Ana pulled out a gift for Vivian. Which turned out to be a purple T-shirt that had the same message in pink on it as the stuffed jaguar had. His heart swelled even more that Ana had thought to get something for Vivian as well. Not that he was surprised. Ana had the biggest heart of anyone he knew.

Some days he could hardly believe he'd ended up with her, that they ran a pack together. That their lives were filled with so much damn love and family.

At the sound of a knock on the front door, Noel jumped up. "That's probably Nathan. And maybe some others. I texted a bunch of the pack with the news. I know I should have asked first but I just got really excited." Her cheeks flushed pink, but she didn't look the least bit apologetic as she ran for the front door.

The truth was, he didn't care that she'd let everyone know. This was his pack, his family. He wanted to celebrate with all of them.

As packmates rushed in, some still in pajamas, everyone wanting to congratulate them, he looked over at his mate, who was practically glowing as she embraced December and talked excitedly about decorating a nursery.

I love you so much it hurts, he told her.

She glanced over at him, her dark eyes shining with a wild love he knew was only going to grow stronger as the years went on. *Right back at you, mate of mine.*

Ana was the mate of his heart, the female he'd loved from the moment they'd met. All those decades separated from her were worth it because it had brought them to this moment, to this life they'd created together. And he planned to protect her and their family for the rest of their very long lives.

Thank you for reading A Mate for Christmas. If you don't want to miss any future releases, please feel free to join my newsletter. Find the signup link on my website: http://www.katiereus.com

ACKNOWLEDGMENTS

It's time to thank my usual crew! I'm grateful to Kari, Julia, Jaycee and Sarah for each part you played in helping me get this book ready for publication! For my family, thank you, thank you, thank you for all your patience with my writing schedule. You guys keep me sane. As always, I'm also grateful to God. To my readers, as you've probably realized, this is the final chapter in the Moon Shifter series. I'm not saying there won't be more in this world someday, but it was time to end this series. I wanted to write something special for you, my wonderful readers, and say goodbye to characters who I love dearly in a way I hope you love as well.

COMPLETE BOOKLIST

Red Stone Security Series
No One to Trust
Danger Next Door
Fatal Deception
Miami, Mistletoe & Murder
His to Protect
Breaking Her Rules
Protecting His Witness
Sinful Seduction
Under His Protection
Deadly Fallout
Sworn to Protect
Secret Obsession
Love Thy Enemy
Dangerous Protector
Lethal Game

Deadly Ops Series
Targeted
Bound to Danger
Chasing Danger (novella)
Shattered Duty
Edge of Danger
A Covert Affair

The Serafina: Sin City Series
First Surrender
Sensual Surrender
Sweetest Surrender
Dangerous Surrender

ABOUT THE AUTHOR

Katie Reus is the *New York Times* and *USA Today* bestselling author of the Red Stone Security series, the Moon Shifter series and the Deadly Ops series. She fell in love with romance at a young age thanks to books she pilfered from her mom's stash. Years later she loves reading romance almost as much as she loves writing it.

However, she didn't always know she wanted to be a writer. After changing majors many times, she finally graduated summa cum laude with a degree in psychology. Not long after that she discovered a new love. Writing. She now spends her days writing dark paranormal romance and sexy romantic suspense.

For more information on Katie please visit her website: www.katiereus.com. Also find her on twitter @katiereus or visit her on facebook at: www.facebook.com/katiereusauthor.

Made in the USA
Lexington, KY
03 July 2018